The

C000294384

The Tempest Twins 6

RUNNER!

John Harvey

Beaver Books

A Beaver Book
Published by Arrow Books Limited
62–5 Chandos Place, London WC2N 4NW

An imprint of Century Hutchinson Ltd

London Melbourne Sydney Auckland
Johannesburg and agencies throughout the world

First published 1988

Set in Baskerville
by JH Graphics Ltd, Reading

Made and printed in Great Britain
by Anchor Brendon Ltd
Tiptree, Essex

ISBN 0 09 958030 6

About the author

John Harvey was born in London and now lives in Nottingham. Most of his time is divided between writing scripts for television and radio and writing fiction. He also runs *Slow Dancer Press*, a small press which concentrates on publishing poetry.

His most recent work for television includes *Sophia and Constance*, a six-part adaptation of Arnold Bennett's *The Old Wives' Tale*, for BBC2. Among his books for younger readers are *What About It, Sharon?* (Puffin Plus); and *Last Summer, First Love* (Pan). His first novel featuring Detective Inspector Charlie Resnick, *Lonely Hearts*, will be published by Viking in 1990.

1

Sam would never be sure what woke him. One moment he lay deep in sleep, the next his eyes were open, his senses alert. The lights of cars passing over Brooklyn Bridge flickered their way across the ceiling. Sam eased himself silently on to one elbow; his brother Lennie's dark hair showed above the edge of white sheet that tangled about him on his bed at the far side of the room. Lennie's breathing, low and even, seemed to be the only sound.

Sam blinked at his watch: twenty minutes after three.

The twins had been tired out after an especially busy evening in the restaurant; in bed shortly after midnight, each had dropped off almost at once.

Until now . . .

Sam slid out from beneath the covers and stood up. His faded blue jeans were within reach and he pulled these on, tucking in the white T-shirt in which he had been sleeping. He moved bare-footed to his brother's bed and shook him by the shoulder, setting one finger immediately against his lips to indicate silence.

Lennie nodded that he understood and sat up, rubbing the corners of his eyes. 'What's up?' he whispered.

'I'm not sure.'

'It'd better be worth it,' Lennie warned.

There were a million and one things that Lennie wasn't too keen on, ranging from French fries smothered in mayonnaise to wearing a shirt and tie, and being woken in the middle of the night for no good reason rated up there with the best of them.

'I think there's somebody downstairs,' said Sam, softly.

Lennie shook his head. 'Of course there is. There's Dad and Alice tucked up in one bed and our beloved stepsister Ruth dreaming of spotty pop stars in another.'

'That wasn't exactly what I meant,' said Sam.

'I'm glad to hear it. Now are you going to tell me what *was*, or do I have to guess?'

Before Sam could reply, they both heard a sound from lower down in the building. More precisely, two sounds: the first a thump, slightly hollow, as if somebody had bumped into something; the second, muffled, was a voice raised in anger or surprise.

The twins' eyes met.

Lennie was on his feet in a single, fluid movement, one hand reaching out to catch the pair of chinos that Sam threw over to him from the pile of discarded clothing beyond the bed end.

'Let's go,' said Sam, soft footing it to the door.

Lennie followed close after him, tapping his brother on the shoulder as they were about to leave the room. 'Hang on,' he said.

The baseball bat had been a present from Howard, their father, two birthdays back. Its surface was dented and scratched with use and it felt heavy and familiar in Lennie's hand. 'What say we hit a few home runs?' he grinned.

8

Sam smiled back and led the way out on to the stairs.

Being a musician, Howard was snoring in the key of C, the notes sliding out beneath the door where he slept with the twins' stepmother. Further along the first floor landing, the door to Ruth's room was slightly ajar and Sam opened it a fraction more. His stepsister seemed to have fallen asleep upside down in the bed, two pillows across the middle of her back. She had her thumb in her mouth and was cuddling both a moth-eaten teddy bear and poster-sized photograph of Michael J. Fox.

'Dream on,' Sam whispered, pulling the door against the frame.

Lennie gestured for him to get a move on from the top of the final flight of stairs. Below, were the dining room of Alice's Riverside Restaurant, the kitchen, and a small room that functioned as Alice's office, and, finally, the customers' toilets.

The twins descended as far as the door and waited, holding their breaths, listening.

There was nothing.

Not a sound other than their own breathing.

Not a . . .

Somewhere beyond the door, wood scraped against wood, the leg of a chair was pushed along the floor as somebody squeezed past it.

Lennie looked at Sam questioningly.

Sam nodded.

Lennie opened the door, fast.

What they saw were tables loaded with upturned chairs, the bare counter of the ice-cream section, the metal of the till by the door catching the reflection of the street lamp on the corner outside.

What they saw was a kid not much more than thirteen, stranded midway between the kitchen and the main entrance. He had a skinny body, made more so by tight black jeans and a dark green-ribbed jumper; his hair had been cut short, and badly, and then spiked up with so much gel it was a wonder he wasn't top heavy. His mouth was open, his dark eyes were stretched wide and he was balancing eight boxed blueberry fruit pies on his arms.

'Hungry, huh?' said Lennie, moving to cut off the kid's escape route to the door.

'Maybe he didn't see the closed sign?' suggested Sam, stepping between the pie thief and the kitchen.

'Maybe he can't read at all?' said Lennie.

'We'll have to teach him a lesson, then,' Sam said, starting to close in on the kid, whose mouth had fallen open and who was beginning to sweat.

'The difference between right and wrong,' said Lennie.

'Thou shalt not steal,' said Sam.

'No such thing,' grinned Lennie, 'as a free lunch.'

'Not even a free night-time snack.'

'Oh, he isn't getting this for free,' said Lennie.

'That's right,' agreed Sam. 'He's going to have to pay.'

'One way or another.'

They were within a few feet of the kid now, and concentrating on him so hard, they didn't hear the movement behind them until it was almost too late. Even then, it needed the shift of focus in the kid's eyes to warn them and make them turn their heads.

If the blueberry pie thief was skinny, his colleague was exactly his opposite. He stood at the open doorway to Alice's office, belly bulging over the belt of his jeans like a sack of potatoes sagging low inside a sweat-stained Iron Maiden T-shirt. One half of his hair had been cropped close to his scalp and sprayed vermilion; the remainder hung down past his shoulder in lank, black strands. In one hand he held the petty-cash tin from the office desk; tightly clasped between the fingers of the other was a knife with a double-edged blade.

Stubble grew like a rash across his face.

His eyes were sunk deep beneath thick eyelashes and they had a strange brightness.

The traffic hummed off the Manhattan end of the bridge and sped into the city. In the middle distance an ambulance siren wailed.

'Put it back,' said Sam, evenly, looking at the cash box.

'Shut your stupid face!' the fat intruder hissed back. He looked a few years older than the twins, around twenty maybe — that and heavier than the two of them put together.

'Put the money back and go,' said Sam.

'Sure,' said Lennie. 'Take the pies and go. Enjoy them on us.'

'Right,' said Sam; 'our treat.'

Something between a laugh and a growl forced its way up from the intruder's throat. 'Hear that, Neb? Their treat.'

The kid choked off a nervous giggle.

'Till a moment back, they weren't going to be giving away no treat, Neb. They were going to beat you into little pieces and put you inside a pie of their own.' He looked at Sam and then at Lennie with the same contempt. 'Now they're up against the two of us they ain't so sure. Ain't so brave. Not when the odds are even.'

'Two of you's nothing,' said Lennie, quick to rise.

'Oh, no?'

'No!'

'So what is?'

'The knife,' said Lennie. 'That's what is.' He was staring at the fat burglar hard, pushing at him, hoping that if he goaded him strongly enough all of the attention would fall on him. Then Sam could make his move.

'You ain't afraid of this little pig sticker, are you? Tough guy like you.'

'I'm not afraid, full stop,' Lennie declared.

Another laugh grumbled its way up into the intruder's throat and this time he punctuated it by spitting on the floor not far in front of Lennie's feet.

Sam judged that he wasn't going to get a better chance. He jumped forward, fast, one hand going for the intruder's right wrist, the other, bunched into a tight fist, aiming for his jaw. The thief realized too slowly what was happening; reacted too late. Sam's fingers closed about his wrist and forced the knife down and to the side, just as his punch struck home to the edge of the chin.

There was a grunt and the intruder stumbled back a couple of paces. It was going to take more than that to put him down.

Lennie had moved a split second after his brother. He had taken three fast paces towards the centre of the restaurant and stiff-armed the skinny kid smack on the side of the face, immediately in front of the ear. The kid had gone back like an eight ball, when it's caught full-flush by the cue. He sailed into the nearest table, making it skid backwards and sending all four stacked chairs bouncing noisily in every

12

direction. Eight blueberry pies spun into the air and smashed down around the kid, several of them scoring direct hits about his face and body. Even the edges of their boxes stung and scratched.

Sam had managed to twist the other burglar's arm almost round to his back, but he still couldn't exert enough pressure to force his fingers open, so that the knife would drop.

'Lennie!' Sam called.

'Yeah?'

'Lend a hand, will you?'

Lennie lent more than a hand. He closed in fast, feinted with a punch to the head, pulled it back at the last moment and settled instead for sinking his knee as deep into the gut as it would go. It was like jumping on a giant pillow from a great height. There was a hiss of bad air and the intruder's mouth opened wide as he doubled forwards.

Lennie sidestepped smartly and lifted both arms high above his head, linking his fingers tight before bringing them down like a guillotine against the back of the intruder's neck.

The fingers of his right hand opened and the knife clattered to the floor. A squeal escaped from his throat.

Sam kicked out and took his legs from beneath him, whereupon Lennie promptly sat on his shoulders, forcing his face fast against the boards.

The kid brushed broken piece of pie from his face and bolted towards the door.

'Hey!' Sam shouted. 'Don't!'

The kid stuttered to a halt and turned his head back towards the centre of the room.

'Just don't!' ordered Sam, in his firmest voice.

13

The kid shrugged. He sat on the floor and slowly licked at the blueberry juice that was trickling down his cheek and running round towards his chin.

'Trouble?' Howard came through the door from above, wearing a blue and white striped dressing gown and a bemused expression.

'No,' said Sam. 'Not really.'

'Not,' grinned Lennie, pushing his captive's face a little harder into the floor, 'any more.'

2

The first police car despatched was detoured to the scene of a shooting in Chinatown and never made it. The second was doing fine until its rear axle fell foul of a pot hole, three feet wide by two deep and had to wait for the repair unit. By the time the third car pulled to a standstill on the cobbled street that led down to Alice's Restaurant, some forty minutes had passed and things inside were pretty well in hand.

The fat intruder who'd threatened the twins with his knife was tied up at the ankles and arms and attached to the large industrial refrigerator in the kitchen. Enquiries had established that his name was Freddy and that he would be back out on the streets just as soon as he got the chance to call his lawyer. Tied up the way he was, Freddy's threats sounded pretty empty. He looked younger, too; probably not a lot more than eighteen, nineteen.

At first he swore a lot, until Alice assured him she'd untie him and then secure him again *inside* the refrigerator, which seemed to calm him down a great deal.

His companion in crime, the skinny Neb, was sitting guiltily at a corner table in the restaurant, gobbling down cherry pie and chocolate ice cream. He would fork a mouthful between thin lips, glance around, swallow fast and then wash it down with a swig of Coke.

'Poor kid doesn't look as though he's had a square meal in ages,' Alice had commented, surveying him.

'"Poor kid",' Howard reminded her, 'was on his way out of here with half the contents of your pie shelf and the petty cash.'

'I know, I know,' Alice said. 'But that was before. Look at him now.'

Howard, Ruth and the twins all stood there and looked.

Neb blushed, choked on some pie, blushed some more, choked again and would quite likely have passed away if Alice had not strode over and thumped him once, hard, in the small of the back. Not for the first time, fragments of pie spewed out all over the floor.

Neb knotted his bony knuckles into his face and began to cry.

Alice gave him a couple of Kleenex and left him alone.

Ruth looked at him with her soppiest smile, as if he was some kind of stray that had wandered in off the street.

Sam looked at his watch and then at Lennie, who was looking at the restaurant clock. 'Just as well this isn't an emergency,' he remarked.

Lennie was agreeing, when they hear the police car braking to a halt outside.

The two officers who came in were in uniform. Jed Chambers was a rookie cop with only two months on the streets to his credit, during which time he had seen more action than in the whole of his life up to that point. Since he had grown up in the backlands of South Dakota, that was hardly surprising. Out there, anything more exciting than a stray steer walking down Main Street was enough to fetch out not just the local sheriff, but the fire brigade as well.

Jed's partner was a black cop with a boxer's face and a head of crisp grey hair that made him look older than his thirty-four years. He was Armstrong Cutler, and at eighteen he'd won the Golden Gloves final at the middleweight limit and some of the papers had been tipping him for a great future in boxing. Maybe a world champ, some had claimed. Maybe. . .

What had happened was that Armstrong got himself signed up to a manager with more ambition than sense, who had pitched him in against the wrong fighters too soon in what proved to be a short and painful career.

Before he was within touch with his twenty-first birthday, Armstrong Cutler had had his nose broken three times, he had two permanently taped ribs and so much scar tissue over his eye that it looked like the topping on a king-sized slice of lemon meringue pie. He had been lucky to get himself knocked out within one minute thirty seconds of stepping out into the ring for what proved to be his last fight. The medical commission had ordered him to retire on the grounds that any further punishment might seriously endanger his health.

So Armstrong had hung up his gloves, and spent three months doing nothing but draw his social security cheque and hang out in the local pool hall. When he got fed up with that, he had worked for a spell as a longshoreman and then in construction, but that had ended when he walked away rather than get into a fight with one of his fellow workers.

'Yellow!' they had called after him.

But Armstrong knew better: he knew his reactions and his strength well enough to realize that, had he wanted, he could have put the man down on the ground with two good shots, one from each fist.

Less than a month after that, Armstrong Cutler had enrolled at the Police Academy and was working at night school to catch up with the education he'd missed. Now he was an experienced street cop, exactly the kind of a man you'd want in your corner when the going got tough — exactly the kind of an older man to teach a rookie like Jed Chambers the ropes.

'Hey,' said Armstrong, 'sorry 'bout the hold up. Busy night out there, I guess.'

'Ain't it always?' said his partner.

'You folks had a burglary?' said Armstrong, addressing his remarks to Alice and Howard.

'Some time back,' said Alice, slightly sharply.

'Like I said, ma'am,' said Armstrong, 'I apologize for . . .'

'That's all right, Officer,' said Howard. 'My wife didn't mean anything by it.'

'Says who?' demanded Alice, turning on him, with fire in her voice and her eyes. 'Who are you to explain what I mean by what I say?'

'Okay,' said Howard, backing off before things got out of hand. He'd seen Alice's temper before and knew what she was like when she boiled over. 'I was only trying to smooth things down.'

'And I was only trying to point out that if it hadn't

been for Sam and Lennie here we might all have been murdered in our beds!'

'Mum!' said Ruth, appalled.

'Alice!' said Howard, reproachfully.

'At least, we might have lost the petty cash,' said Alice.

'Not to mention eight blueberry specials,' added Lennie with a grin.

'What is missing, ma'am?' Armstrong enquired.

'Nothing.'

'Nothing at all?'

'Not a thing.'

Armstrong looked over at his younger partner, who was eyeing what remained of the cherry pie that the terrified Neb no longer had the courage to eat. 'Seems like things ain't so urgent after all, then, ma'am,' he said.

'Thanks to these boys here,' said Alice. 'If they hadn't dealt with these hoodlums themselves, it wouldn't have been any use waiting for you to come and catch them, would it? It being such a busy night and all!'

And with that Alice swept off and pushed through the double doors into the kitchen. Jed saw any chance he might have had of getting a free portion of pie, maybe even a cup of coffee, going with her. Armstrong, who knew the night shift well enough to carry a giant Thermos in the car with him, wasn't too worried about coffee. What he wanted to do now was get the incident written up, statements signed and witnessed, then haul the two perpetrators out of there before something more urgent called them away.

'By the way, sir,' he said to Howard, 'it said on the call we got that two perpetrators were involved.

Assuming that this shrimp here is one of them, where might we find the other one?'

'In the kitchen,' said Howard.

'You're not feeding him, too?' asked Jed Chambers, who was starting to feel that the bad guys were getting the best deal around here.

Howard shook his head. 'More like freezing him,' he said. 'At least, keeping him on ice.'

'That's fine,' said Armstrong, with a nod of his grizzled head. 'In that case, why don't these boys here take a seat and give us an account of what happened. Then we can take it from there.'

Sam and Lennie nodded and went ahead, while Howard went off into the kitchen to see if Alice was calm enough to offer the two cops some of her best espresso.

By the time the paperwork was finished it was close to dawn. The first shift of customers — those who worked on the nearby fish dock — would be coming in for their breakfasts and another working day would have begun. Armstrong and Jed would have hauled their prisoners off to the holding cells and gone home to their respective apartments and tried to sleep through as many of the daylight hours as they could manage.

'You did a good job, son,' said Armstrong to Lennie, shaking him by the hand. 'You both did.'

He shook Sam's hand, also — a good, firm grip that didn't need to prove it owner's strength.

'That scrawny two-bits' worth a man'd only have to blow at for him to fall down, but that other guy, that Freddy, he's a different piece of work altogether.'

'He's known to you, then?' asked Lennie.

'He's got a rap sheet takes the computer some time

to spread it all across the screen: burglary; assault; demanding money with menaces; threatening behaviour; he's one nasty dude.'

'If he's that bad and the police know about it,' said Sam, 'how come he's still at liberty?'

'Sonny,' said Armstrong, 'you're in danger of taking after your mother a shade too much for my liking.'

'She's my stepmother,' Sam corrected him.

'Sorry, I'm sure.'

'Not that I mind taking after her — where some things are concerned.'

Armstrong shrugged. 'To answer your question,' he said, after a moment, 'maybe the courts are too lenient, I ain't to say. Could be he's on probation, right now. Then again, could be no one's ever got him bang to rights before.'

'You think that's what he is now?' asked Lennie; 'bang to rights?'

Armstrong looked over at his partner.

'We've got latent prints on the cash box,' said Jed Chambers, 'also on the desk. Prints on the knife with which the two of you are prepared to stand up under oath and swear Freddy used towards you in a threatening manner. There are probably more prints out back where he pushed the kid through the bathroom window to gain entry. Also, if we can convince that kid he ought to be more frightened of us than he is of Freddy, he might give evidence against him too. If all of that isn't enough, I don't know what is? Right, Armstrong?'

'Maybe,' Armstrong nodded. 'Just don't hold your breath.'

Sam and Lennie watched as first Neb and then the

handcuffed Freddy were pushed into the police car. Before Jed could shut the door on him, Freddy turned his head angrily towards the twins and glared.

He didn't say a word, but he didn't need to. What he was thinking was written on his face, plain as the new day that was dawning: if and when I get on the streets again, watch out, the pair of you, because I'm going to be coming after you — and next time it won't be so easy!

3

The entire top floor of the building belonged to the twins — at least, for as long as they chose to live there it did.

Their parents had divorced some time back and Sam and Lennie had finished secondary schooling in England. Not long after their sixteenth birthday, they had taken a trans-atlantic jet from Heathrow to the John F. Kennedy airport in New York and begun a new life — just as their father, Howard, had done earlier.

Howard had taken Alice as a second wife (or, more likely, given her temper and temperament, she had taken him) and the twins had taken her as a step-mother. Sam had put his chance of going on into further education on hold for the present and as for Lennie, well, Lennie had pretty much had it with books and classes and all of that kind of thing anyhow.

Right now, they were learning about life and living close to the centre of the world's fastest and most energetic city taught a person real fast. They worked in the restaurant in order to earn enough spending money and spent their spare time enjoying whatever was going on around them and trying to keep out of trouble — or, as Alice would have put it, trying to get *into* trouble.

Well, was it their fault a couple of passing burglars took a fancy to the place in the middle of the night?

Of course if wasn't.

Sam was sitting cross-legged on the floor alongside his bed. He was wearing a pair of loose, grey, tracksuit bottoms and a deep red sweat shirt; the headphones from his personal stereo were over his ears, the volume turned down low and the tape playing was the unaccompanied cello music of Bach. If Lennie had known he would doubtless have had something sarcastic to say about wasting the time listening to singing dogs. But Lennie was fast asleep after returning from an eight mile late-night run around Manhattan.

Glancing across the room towards his brother, Sam envied him. Ever since they'd been eighteen months old, Lennie had been the one who had slept through the night without waking. Whereas Sam had fretted and cried and only later, when he'd outgrown those things, had he realized that not being able to sleep at night didn't give you the right to keep others awake. So now, when his brain refused to stop working at the appropriate time, he sat upright, listened to music and read. Having got through all of Dickens' novels twice and some three times, he'd decided it was time for a change — and being in America suggested to him that he read something American. Nothing daunted, he had started at the top with Herman Melville's *Moby Dick*: 727 pages (in the Norton Critical Edition) including notes, essays and a selection of Melville's letters.

All that for a dumb whale! Lennie had jeered.

Sam thought that, as a critic, Lennie sucked!

He was already up to chapter 42 and loving it. As he sat there in the comparative darkness, the only source of direct light the small spot he'd rigged up over his bed, Sam lost himself in the sound of the bow being drawn backwards and forwards across the strings of the cello and the description of the vast ocean that was home to the white whale: 'an unbounded prairie sheeted with driven snow'.

Goose pimples crept slowly along the length of Sam's arms and a cold hollow scooped at his stomach. He was still looking at the printed page but the lines were a blur of regular markings; they were like furrows ploughed the length of a vast field that pushed back and back against the horizon.

For some little time Sam knew he was no longer thinking of the white whale, but he did not know where his imagination had taken him. But then the music came to an end, the tape clicked off into sudden, total silence and he knew: in his mind he was somewhere he had never been, he was in the vastness of Montana, the prairies of Big Sky Country.

He was thinking of Marcie.

The first time Sam had seen her, Marcie was just a girl around his own age with a torn blue T-shirt and bright green eyes. Later he found out that she'd run away from home, out west in Montana, and hitched her way to New York. She'd been looking for freedom, fortune and (though she would never have admitted it) love. What she'd found had been none of those things. There she was, barely sixteen, living rough, picking pockets and losing hope. It finally got to the point where she knew she couldn't hang on in New York and she knew there was no way she was going to go back to her folks in Montana.

Sam had found her hanging by her arms from the iron safety railing out above a section of busy motorway. Twenty metres below her swinging legs, cars roared back and forth over hard concrete.

Sam had climbed up and then shimmied his way towards her, metre by terrifying metre. Sweat had clogged his armpits, clung to the middle of his back and between his legs. It had made his eyes sting; had meant that all he could see of Marcie was a blur of hands and arms and hair.

Sam's heart had stopped when he saw one of those hands pull away and release its hold on the rail, on life.

'Don't do that!' he had yelled.

'Why the hell not?' Marcie had yelled back.

'It frightens the life out of me.'

Marcie had laughed. 'Out of you?'

'What difference,' she had asked him, 'does it make to you if I live or die?'

'A lot,' Sam had replied, softly. 'More than I could say right now.'

More than he had been able to say then; more than he had been able to say ever.

He had persuaded Marcie to come down safely and the juvenile court had sentenced her to twelve months' probation, with the condition that she go back to her parents. So Marcie had waited for them at the Greyhound Bus Station, along with her probation officer, and when two middle-aged people had climbed off the bus, eyes blinking at the unfamiliar city, Marcie had scarcely recognized them as her mother and father.

They had held her with calloused hands and kissed her with hard, wind-cracked lips and, after a paper cup of coffee and a sugar coated doughnut, all three had got back aboard the bus and rode it all the way back to Great Falls, Montana.

'How old are you, Marcie? How many years have you got waiting for you if you want them? If you want them enough. Marcie, maybe you did see something in me, something you thought you could trust. I hope so, because that's why I'm here. I know that I saw something special in you. I know I want to help you if you'll give me the chance.'

Sam could remember the wind tugging coldly at his face and hands and the way his voice had shaken; the tears that had streamed down Marcie's face as she had reached out to him for help.

Something she could trust?

After six months a postcard had arrived, marked 'Great Falls'. On the front had been a colour picture of a huge prairie, rolling back and back until it met a range of high, snow-capped mountains. On the back of the card, in a scrawled hand, was written: 'This is where I am. Look hard and you'll see me.'

Sam had stared at the card for hour after hour, yet still there was not a soul, not a person to be seen: 'an unbounded prairie sheeted with driven snow'.

Sam set aside his book and walked to the window: the lights in the skyscrapers lit up floor after floor; red, amber, green, blue, the changing colours of the street reflected up towards his gaze. The city was never quiet, never still. Voices raised in anger, in celebration rose up to him. Sirens, and a squeal of tyres.

27

Sam's forehead rested against the cool glass. Out there were so much life and hope, unhappiness and despair; and where was Marcie?

'You know what?' said Lennie, through a mouthful of breakfast pancake.

'No, what?' replied Sam, setting his coffee cup down in its saucer.

'You'll never believe this, but last night I had this stupid dream. On and on.'

Sam poured maple syrup on to the top of his short stack of pancakes and watched with satisfaction as it began to drizzle down.

'What about?' Sam asked.

'That was the weird thing. You remember that girl you talked down off the motorway? Well, it was all about her. What's her name? Yeah, that's it: Marcie.'

Lennie forked some bacon into his mouth alongside the pancake. 'Marcie,' he repeated with a shake of the head. 'Why d'you suppose I dreamed about her?'

4

The singer at the microphone was midway through her second number of the evening and already she was wishing that it was her last. Close up to the horseshoe-shaped stage a party of fertiliser salesmen in town for a convention were whooping it up over pitcher after pitcher of beer. Away to the side, two make-believe cowboys were arm wrestling one another while a small crowd stood around, hollered and laid bets on the outcome. All along the far wall, between the entrance and the cloakrooms, a dozen one-armed bandits were in constant use.

The singer gripped the mike stand a little more tightly and lifted her voice in competition with all that was going on around her. The members of the band, five-strong, exchanged knowing glances, shrugged and carried on playing: Friday night at a third-rate club in Great Falls, Montana — what else could anyone expect?

The singer expected people to listen.

Some of them . . .

'Aching for my sweet baby's arms,' she sang.

'Feeling like an east-bound train,' she sang.

'Ain't no place left but lonely,' she sang: 'No words that don't mean goodbye.'

One of the salesmen called out a remark to a

passing waitress and his friends roared with laughter. Then the waitress turned and poured a bottle of beer over his head and they all laughed a lot more.

Damn it! thought the singer. Those are my words, that's my song; I wrote that and I know it's worth more than that.

Somewhere, out of sight, another waitress slipped on the wet floor and a trayful of drinks went crashing.

The singer stopped mid-chorus. Her head swung back. She pushed an arm high into the air and behind her the band dwindled to a slow, uneasy silence.

'You know,' she said into the microphone; 'you know, I have sung to some trash in my time, but you are the worst, the most no-hope, no-account bunch of know-nothings I have ever seen. You're drunk, you're noisy, you're about as intelligent as a litter straight off the sow and you got the class of a herd of jackasses celebrating Fourth of July!'

One or two of the band made moves to protect their instruments.

The singer hung on to the mike stand with both hands and stared out through the spotlight.

Nobody need have worried: nobody heard more than a couple of words she said.

The arm-wrestling contest came to an end and the winner was helped on to the table by his friends and started to brandish his muscles through the material of his cotton checked shirt.

The singer turned on her heel and strode through the band towards the back of the stage, taking a swipe at one of the drummer's cymbals on the way. It came down with a crash and punctured the top skin of his snare drum, rolling away towards the floor.

By the time it had landed with a final crash, the

singer was back inside the dressing room and the door was locked.

She stood with her head leaning forward against the cracked mirror. Her make-up was blotched with sweat and now tears ran irregular little trails of black down from her eyelashes. Her hair was cut short and died a tawny red. The shirt that stuck to her back was thin yellow cotton with a pink cactus rose embroidered over the left-side breast pocket. Her jeans were faded 501s, tucked into a pair of knee-length white boots with three-inch heels.

After some minutes she opened her eyes. Her breath had blurred circles of mist over the silvered glass.

'Look at yourself, girl,' she said aloud. 'Just take a good look at yourself and tell me what you see.'

If either Sam or Lennie had seen her there in that small, fly-blown room, it is doubtful if they would have recognized her.

She looked angry and empty. She looked as tired as any human being has the right to be. She looked sixteen going on twenty-nine.

'Marcie!'

She blinked at the pounding on the dressing-room door.

'Marcie, you okay in there?'

In the mirror, her eyes forced a smile.

'Let me in now. Come on now, Marcie. Just open up this door.'

She shook her head and sat down in front of the glass, reaching for a box of tissues with which to begin cleaning up her face. There were other voices outside the door now; she could hear them without knowing what it was they were saying. Carefully, she wiped around her eyes. The banging on the door became more insistent, the voices more urgent.

'Marcie! Don't you do nothing foolish, you hear?'

For an answer, she scooped an empty glass from the side and hurled it against the wall alongside the door.

'Marcie!'

They started to use their shoulders against the door then, and by the third charge it had begun to crack down the frame. Marcie sighed and went over and slipped back the bolt; turned the key. When the door was pushed open, the half-dozen faces that stared in at her seemed almost disappointed that she was still all in one piece.

'What in God's name you doing, locking yourself in like that?' one demanded.

'Ain't a lady got a right to a little privacy?' she asked.

'No one, and especially no lady's, got a right to talk to my customers the way you just done,' said the club owner. He was a short man with fake diamonds on his shirt collar, shining from the rings on his fingers and from the monogrammed buckle of his belt. 'I just hope you're sorry for what you just up and done, 'cause you better be, on account it cost you your job!'

'But . . .' began one of the others.

'But nothing!' said the owner fiercely and turned away.

Marcie shrugged and went back to cleaning herself up. Soon the only other person there was Charley Mack, whose band it was and who played fiddle and peddle guitar.

Charley Mack had been the one to discover her, when Marcie had been working in the local Woolworth, singing along to the records that got played over the speaker system and only pausing to make remarks about what the customers were wearing. He had persuaded her to come over and sit in with the band, an audition by any other name, and he'd offered her work one night a week for sure, and a couple of others, maybe.

Marcie had been more than a little doubtful, but it was better than standing at the back of a counter selling a lot of things nobody wanted. After a couple of months she had started writing her own songs instead of singing other people's and Charley Mack had helped her with the music. He'd seemed real proud of her in fact and claimed that she was coming along so well it made him feel like a father to her, but there was something about the look that came into Charley's eye from time to time that made Marcie think his ideas about her weren't exactly fatherly.

Not that he ever laid a hand upon her: he was bright enough to know what he'd get if ever he did.

He watched her now, not saying a thing, went away and returned a few minutes later with a cup of black coffee for Marcie and a bourbon and water for himself. Charley sat there drinking, waiting for Marcie to think of what she wanted to say. Even to look at him would be something, instead of staring into that old mirror all the time.

'What?' Marcie finally blurted out, turning her face towards him fast.

'You know what.'

'What?'

'What you have to go and do a thing like that for?'

'Like what?'

'Getting yourself fired.'

'Because.'

'Because ain't good enough.'

'Nothing ain't good enough now, Charley. Not for me. Not here.'

'It was a bad night, is all.'

Marcie shook her head. 'Charley, they're all bad nights.'

'Kid . . .'

'Don't!'

'Darlin' . . .'

'I ain't nobody's darlin', not yours nor anyone else's.'

'Marcie, then . . .'

'What?'

'You're still short of your seventeenth birthday, how can you be saying all your nights are bad? You got your future ahead of you, you know that, don't you?'

Marcie got up quickly, she took a couple of paces into the room and looked Charley in the face. 'I seen my future tonight, Charley. I come back in here and there it was waiting for me in that mirror.'

'You know it don't have to be that way.'

'If I stay here, it does.'

'Oh, don't you pay no mind to him. Come next weekend he'll have changed his mind and you can carry on just like nothing ever happened.'

'But it has happened, Charley. That's just the point. It has happened.'

'What has?'

'I've made up my mind.'

Charley shook his head with a wry laugh, dry and humourless. 'Okay, out with it.'

'Charley, you reckon I'm pretty good. You said so enough.'

'And so you are.'

'Maybe so. For myself I ain't sure yet. I think I can sing a pretty fair song and I can write one, too. But working dumps like this ain't going to prove nothing. Not one in a dozen listens to what I'm singing anyway.'

'So what you fixing to do about that?'

'What I'm fixing to do is go somewhere where I can find out if I got any talent or not, that's what.'

Charley stood up. 'Oh, Lord! Girl, you going off into the great blue yonder in search of fame and fortune, ain't you?'

'Well why not, 'cause I sure ain't going to find neither of them here.'

Charley was standing close beside her more quickly than she'd thought possible. 'You know there's them here as cares a lot for you, Marcie. What you want to go off and leave all that behind for? Chasing after something that might never happen.'

His right hand was touching Marcie's arm, the fingers pressing against the skin.

'Let me alone, Charley!'

'Honey, I . . .'

'Charley!'

He looked down at her with dark eyes and a slightly uncertain expression. At around six foot he was a head taller than her and he had to be twice her weight. He could have picked her up with one hand and held her above his head. 'I said . . .'

'And I heard you.'

Charley let his hand fall back by his side; with a nod he moved towards the door. 'If ever you change your mind . . .'

'Shut the door behind you, Charley. I still got to get changed.'

She didn't turn her head to look at him, just waited for the sound of the door closing. When it did, she took a swallow at the coffee, exchanged the yellow shirt she'd been on stage in for one with red and blue checks, grabbed her scuffed leather jacket from the back of the door and walked out through the main body of the club.

Nobody noticed her go.

Marcie's mother had risen at six o'clock every morning of her life — every morning she could remember. There was always work to do and never time to waste. In winter the first thing she did was to light the fires, check the boiler and make sure none of the pipes had frozen over. In summertime, she began feeding the animals straight away, and then prepared breakfast for her family — which was now down to two, her husband and her youngest daughter, Marcie.

Breakfast was coffee, wholewheat toast and home-made jam, together, winter and summer, with a bowlful of Cream of the West cereal. This was made from bran, farina and wheatgerm and had the advantage of tasting as good (or as bad) when made with water as with milk. Added to which, it was manufactured right there in the State, over at Billings. And Marcie's mother always thought (and said, whenever she got the chance) that Montana folk should buy Montana products when they could.

So, on that morning the same as any other, some minutes short of seven, the cereal, toast and coffee ready, she went to call Marcie and tell her to hurry on down.

The blankets and top sheet were folded neatly back

36

along the mattress, what few books Marcie owned were straight and ordered on her shelves. A stack of records by Patsy Cline had been put back into their sleeves and were leaning against the record player. Marcie's posters and the few odd and fading photographs she kept tacked to the side of her wardrobe were still there, but when her mother turned the key to the wardrobe door, she saw right away that half of the clothes were missing. Those which remained, however, hung straight on their hangers. All in all, Marcie's mother had never seen her daughter's room and its contents so neatly arranged. Normally, Marcie preferred to live surrounded by chaos. But then, of course, Marcie wasn't living there any more, was she? She had left her room that way on purpose, like a final setting to rights of her life in Great Falls.

The first time she had run away from home, it had been an instant decision, brought on by a loud and tearful argument. This was different: this was considered, logical.

Marcie's mother stood in the centre of the room, aware that she was afraid, uncertain whether that fear was mostly for herself or for Marcie. After a few minutes, she went back downstairs.

Her husband glanced up from behind his bowl of Cream of the West. 'Not getting up?' he mumbled.

'Oh, she's up,' said Marcie's mother, tending to the coffee. Her husband always drank his black, with too much sugar. 'She was up before me.' She placed the cup and saucer down alongside his right arm. 'Up and gone.'

He looked at her through grey and watery eyes, letting the force of her words sink gradually into his mind. 'Gone?' he echoed finally.

'Yep. She's gone.'

Her husband went back to his breakfast, chewing at his cereal slowly, sipping his black, sweet coffee. She buttered herself some toast, added milk to her own coffee, and listened to a truck changing gear close to the house then accelerating away towards the outskirts of the town. Heading where?

For a moment, she had an image of Marcie standing out by some service station, bag at her feet, thumb angled into the air, hitching herself a lift.

Heading where?

As soon as the image faded, Marcie's mother turned her attention back to finishing her breakfast. There were always a million and one things to do and she couldn't afford to sit there all morning wasting time.

5

Lennie was stripped to the waist, sweat running freely from his shoulder blades and moving down along the channel of his spine; his thick, dark hair clung to his scalp, darkened to the blackness of a raven's wing.

Eighty-eight.

Eighty-nine.

Ninety.

Ninety-

'Lennie! Hey, Lennie!' Ruth came into the room like a pimply destroyer in search of prey.

Concentration shot, head turning involuntarily toward the door, Lennie's right arm buckled, his balance failed him and he collapsed on to his side with a groan of anger.

'Lennie, I . . .'

'Damn it, Ruth!'

'There's someone . . .'

'How many times have you got to be told?'

'Someone downstairs . . .'

'You do *not* come into this room without knocking! And I said; *"Not!"*'

'But this is important.'

'So is getting to a hundred.'

'Why? What's a hundred stupid push-ups anyway?'

'Ninety-nine more than you can do, for one!'

'Lennie, for someone your age, you're just a little pathetic, you know that?'

'And for someone your age, pipsqueak, you're more than a little precocious.'

'Whatever that means.'

'Go swallow a dictionary!'

'Go sit on your head!'

'Go squeeze all your spots and drown!'

'Go push yourself up against a truck!'

'Go . . . !'

'Hey, Lennie.' Sam's voice interrupted the slanging match and he lifted Ruth bodily out of the way, setting her down in the corner close to the stereo.

'Yeah?'

'I sent Ruth to tell you.'

'Great! So it's you I've got to thank.'

'For what?'

'For spoiling his precious press-ups,' interrupted Ruth, scornfully.

'Push-ups!' Lennie retorted.

'Look,' said Sam, spreading his arms for calm. 'Can't you two have this out later?'

'I don't want to have anything out with her/him!' Ruth and Lennie protested in unison.

'All right, all right. Never speak to one another again if that's what you want.'

'Fine!' chorused Lennie and Ruth.

'Right now,' Sam said to his brother. 'We're wanted below. Urgent. Okay?'

'Sure,' Lennie shrugged. 'Okay. Why didn't you say so sooner?' And he grabbed at a towel and followed Sam to the stairs, mopping surplus sweat away as he went.

* * *

40

They were the same police officers as before. Armstrong Cutler was standing next to the twins' father, chatting easily about the chances of the new heavyweight boxing hope. They didn't appear to be good. Jed Chambers was trying to describe the Badlands of Dakota to Alice and was getting his tongue tied in knots. Both officers were drinking ice-cold Cokes.

They broke off their conversations as politely as they could when Sam and Lennie came into the restaurant. Passing the time was pleasant enough, but that's all it was. They had a job to do.

'Someone wants to meet you,' Armstrong said, nodding at the twins.

'We're your escort,' added Jed.

Sam looked at Lennie, questioningly; Lennie shrugged his shoulders and made a face that said, roughly, 'Why not?'

'Okay,' said Sam. 'When do we go?'

The officers drained their glasses. 'Now.'

Armstrong Cutler thanked Alice for her hospitality and she told them they were welcome to stop by any time their work brought them that way. Howard let it be known that if a spare ticket for the big fight at Madison Square Garden came the policeman's way, he would be interested in taking it off his hands.

Armstrong nodded, promised to do what he could and, for the present, took his sons off his hands instead.

Outside, Jed Chambers was already behind the wheel of the police vehicle, revving the engine lightly with the sole of his shoe.

The softball field set in the centre of Central Park

was guarded around one section by a length of high chain-mail fence. If one of the pitchers sent down a fast ball which eluded both the batter and the catcher it was unlikely to fell an innocent passer-by.

There were benches arranged at intervals at the edge of the path so that spectators could watch the games in comfort. That afternoon there was one game in progress and the players for a second were warming up on a nearby pitch.

The benches held an assortment of bag ladies and winos, a mother endlessly rocking the handle of her baby's pram, and a woman sitting on her own eating pistachio nuts. She was in her late thirties to look at her; she wore blue jeans that hadn't yet had the chance to fade, a white sweat shirt without a single logo or advertisement anywhere on it, and a grey and white speckled cap, the peak of which shaded her eyes against the sun.

Jed Chambers parked his car on one of the park's wide paths and Armstrong Cutler pushed open the rear door. 'There you go,' he said.

'Where?' asked Sam; 'I mean, exactly.'

Armstrong pointed towards the bench where the woman was keeping the sun from her eyes and breaking open nuts with her thumbnail.

'Anyone we should know?' Lennie asked.

'Hey!' said the grey-haired police officer. 'We brought you out here, now why don't you go do the rest for yourselves?'

Sam and Lennie walked away from the car, which drove smartly away, weaving between the many roller skaters and joggers who were earnestly circling the park.

The woman slipped another nut into her mouth

42

and kept resolutely looking through the fence at a chubby youth in a red and white striped T-shirt who was desperately trying to hit a home run.

'Hi, guys!' she said, cheerily, as soon as the twins were close.

'Lieutenant?' said Sam, cautiously, half-recognizing the voice.

'Take a seat, why don't you?'

Sam sat one side of her, Lennie the other. The batter struck the ball high but wide and it soared out of play way off to the right.

'Tough break!'

'What's the idea?' asked Lennie.

Lieutenant Jackie Eves had been involved, one way or another, in most of the twins' New York adventures. She'd hauled them out of dangerous scrapes and they had assisted her and the men and women of her precinct in a number of difficult cases. They trusted one another, that was the bottom line: they even liked each other. But what was this all about?

'You on holiday, Lieutenant?' Lennie asked.

'Not exactly,' she replied, easing the peak of her cap away from her eyes a little. 'And you better call me Jackie.'

'Well,' said Lennie, 'that's nice of you, Lieu . . .'

'Jackie,' she said, more forcefully.

'Right. Got you, Jackie.'

'The pair of you,' she added, turning her attention towards Sam.

'Sure,' nodded Sam. 'You don't want people to know you're with the police department, right?

'Right.'

'Oh-oh,' said Lennie. 'You mean you're undercover?'

'You could say that,' Jackie Eves said.

'As of now,' Lennie pursued. 'This minute?'

The lieutenant nodded.

Both of the twins couldn't help looking around them for something or somebody suspicious.

'Relax! The only criminal thing going down around here right now is the way that guy out there is pitching.' She smiled. 'This just seemed like a pretty neutral place to meet with you guys. Besides, it's a nice day out, isn't it?'

The twins nodded and waited; whatever the lieutenant had in mind she would tell them in her own time.

After a few minutes, Jackie Eves screwed up the empty bag in which she had been nurturing the last of her pistachio nuts, pushed it down into the pocket of her jeans and stood up. 'I'm about through here. What say we take a walk! I'll buy you guys a Coke or something.'

'Sure,' said Sam.

'Sure,' said Lennie.

Jackie Eves grinned and led the way past the chain fence towards the small lake where little kids gathered around the statue of Hans Christian Andersen to listen to stories. Which, in a way, was what Sam and Lennie were going to do — it was just a different kind of story.

'I don't have to tell the two of you about the problems we've got here in the city with drugs.'

They were sitting on the grass a dozen or so feet back from the path that ran round the lake. The lieutenant sipped at a 7-Up as she talked; Sam and Lennie drank their Cokes. On the lake a marooned model motor boat refused to return to its owner.

44

'A lot of our street crime, a lot of petty theft and burglary is drug related; people who've got this or that habit and who need money in order to buy supplies and fix. Some of these are your age, some a lot younger. I've seen twelve, thirteen year olds with needle marks all over their bodies. That and a whole lot of other things I'm not going to talk about, on account I just don't want to have to think about them again.'

Sam and Lennie nodded, listening.

'I'm not saying that the drug problem has got worse, but it's changing and in ways we don't like. Up till a year or so back, it was pretty much under the thumb of organized crime . . .'

'You mean the Mafia?' Lennie interrupted.

'Call it what you like. They had a way of doing things that kept the lid down pretty tight and they controlled their own. Anyone tried a double-cross or attempted to muscle in on the action, they dealt with them quick and simple. Not pretty, I'll grant you, but quick and simple.'

Jackie Eves paused and looked out across the lake; the model boat was now, slowly but certainly, sinking. 'Now what you got is crack. It's a drug that's easy to make, easy to sell. You don't need a great organization to bring it halfway across the world. And because it's cheaper on the streets than a lot of other drugs, it's getting more kids hooked than ever.

'You get yourself a gun and, say, twenty thousand dollars and overnight you're in big business. Instead of one outfit now there are dozens of them. Only the street won't take that many and pretty soon they turn on one another and start trying to take each other out of the game. That means lots of gun play, lots of innocent people, lots of cops getting hurt. Worse;

45

getting killed. I lost two officers from my precinct within half an hour of one another last week. Both of them shot at close range, one in the face.'

Anger showed clearly in the lieutenant's eyes.

'So I'm going undercover for a spell with a task force from Narcotics. We've got two aims: the first is to stop the number of crack dealers spreading; the second is to find a way of preventing so many youngsters from getting hooked on the stuff in the first place.'

She took a breath and looked first at Sam, then at Lennie, finally back at Sam again. 'I need help.'

The twins exchanged glances; both were aware that the skin along their arms had turned to goose bumps. Already their throats were dry.

'I've been able to do a few things for you in the past — right now I want to call in a few favours.'

Jackie Eves looked at them again, gauging their response. As for the twins, their minds were racing, trying to figure out what it was the police woman had in mind.

'I'll go into details later,' Jackie Eves said, 'but for now, in principle, what do you say?'

'We say, "Sure!"' said Lennie, without hesitation. 'Don't we, Sam?'

Sam didn't rush his answer; but then, unless it was absolutely necessary, Sam didn't rush into anything without giving it some serious thought.

He gave this three minutes and twenty seconds — which, when you're waiting for someone to speak, seems like a very long time.

When he did open his mouth, however, there was an accompanying smile in his blue eyes. 'All right, Jackie. Whatever you think we can do to help — we'll do it.'

6

There was no way, of course, for Marcie to know this, but she was close to where the New York rookie cop, Jed Chambers, had been born. She was in a truck, a battered Buick, travelling east on Highway 18 and they had just driven through the town of Oglala in a spume of white dust. If the driver had taken it into his head to swerve off to the north and follow the narrow road that moved alongside the Porcupine River, he would have arrived at Sharps Corner. This small South Dakota town was where Jed Chambers' parents still lived — not only his mother and father, but two elder brothers and a sister who was five years younger. There on the edge of the Pine Ridge Indian Reservation, not so many miles away from the site of the Wounded Knee Massacre — in which the American troops had mown down large numbers of helpless American Indians — Jed had grown from a stocky little kid with a pugnacious temper into a teenager who seemed to have shot up overnight into a beanpole with broad shoulders. In fact, the only thing about him that didn't seem to have changed was his temper.

Of course, sitting as far along the bench seat of the truck as she could, Marcie knew none of this. She knew nothing about any New York cop called

Chambers or anything else. She didn't have any idea there was any place called Sharps Corner and, chances were, that if she had, she wouldn't have thought it was worth spitting on.

What Marcie did know was that she didn't like the driver one bit and she trusted him even less. After you'd hitched around as much as Marcie you got a second sense about who to trust and who to steer clear of. When she saw this man leaning down from his truck window, kind of leering at her with that wall-eyed look, everything inside her told her to shake her hand at him and step back from the edge of the highway. But she had already been waiting there, close to the Wyoming-South Dakota border for close to two hours and it was beginning to get dark. Not only dark, but cold. The coat she'd brought with her was scarcely enough to keep out the wind that was cutting down from the north-east.

It'll be okay, she had told herself as she went around and climbed into the truck. Keep well out of his reach, say as little as possible. Most import-ant, don't let on how far you're travelling. Any minute things look as if they might become the least bit dangerous, you simply say, 'Hey, fine, mister! This is where I get off!'

If it was that straightforward, Marcie thought now, why am I still so worried? Why indeed?

The driver squinted in her direction and reached down into the ice box he kept on the floor close to his feet. He took out a can of beer and offered it to Marcie, who shook her head and declined.

'Suit yourself,' he shrugged.

He tugged away the metal ring and tossed it over his shoulder, so that it bounced off the nude woman

smiling out from the calendar that hung there. 'Bulls-
eye!' he laughed, and proceeded to swallow down the
beer at a fast rate.

Choke youself! Marcie thought, and swung her
head away to stare out at the expanse of land that
faded into a darkening horizon.

Marcie's father never had a lot to say for himself at the
best of times and this was far from the best of times.

Ever since his wife had told him that morning that
Marcie had run off, he had been unable to get certain images out of his mind. Marcie on the occasion
of her third birthday, wearing that new red dress with
white lace they'd saved for and bought from a
neighbour's catalogue. Marcie when she was twelve,
sitting with a guitar in her lap and her brow all fur-
rowed up as she tried to figure out which fingers to
press down on which strings. Marcie looking up suddenly at her High School picnic, surprised and smiling. A faded image, the oldest of them all, of himself
— barely recognizable as a younger man — holding
a week-old baby girl cradled in his arms. That was
Marcie, too.

Now she was gone.

He worked through the day slowly, letting the
pictures from the past fall down, one in front of the
other. Working slowly and not speaking to anyone.

The Buick had pulled into a service station at the
intersection of Highway 18 and Highway 73. The
driver had had the tank filled, water and oil checked
and had told Marcie he was going over for a cup of
coffee and something to eat. She could come along
with him or stay where she was, suit herself.

Marcie didn't have money to spare but the thought of food brought all the hunger she'd been ignoring flooding to her senses. She *had* to get something to eat.

As she followed the driver across the cinder lot towards the Bear-in-the-Lodge Diner, she made up her mind that she'd look around inside for someone else she could hitch a ride with.

The neon lights of the diner were blue and it was dark enough for them to be shining brightly. The juke box was playing a Patsy Cline record as they went in and Marcie automatically began singing along with it.

'Hey, kid!' said the driver, as they sat down. 'You ain't got half bad a voice.'

Marcie shut up.

The driver shrugged, rolled himself a cigarette without offering her the makings, and when the waitress rolled over to them, he ordered coffee, black, a steak, well-done, with fries and tomatoes, a slice of peach pie with cream and a beer. Marcie checked the menu, checked the change in her pocket and settled for a cheeseburger and a glass of water.

'Big spender!' said the waitress.

Marcie looked up at her with a sudden angry feeling. She wanted to tell her to mind her own business; wanted to ask her if she knew her lipstick was smudged across her front teeth; wanted to tell her how stupid she looked wearing a dress that was two sizes too small for her, making her look like a blow-up doll with a bad blonde wig.

She said none of those things.

'Talkative, ain't you?' said the driver.

Marcie shot him a look that warned him to shut up.

The man laughed in her face.

When the cheeseburger came it was greasy and only barely warm and the bun was so stale that it was like chewing on second-hand cardboard. The water was warm and the glass bore an interesting selection of finger prints. She glanced across at the driver, who was shaking a mass of tomato sauce over his steak and smothering his fries with chilli relish.

'Great food!' he enthused, through a mouthful of meat and potato.

Marcie pushed her plate aside and went to the ladies' room. She took her time on the way there, looking the place over for a possible replacement driver, but the other men either had someone with them, or else looked too young or too drunk.

She took her time, hoping that he would get fed up with waiting and leave her stranded, so making the decision for her. But when she walked back into the diner there he was chatting to the waitress by the cash desk. As soon as he saw her he waved her over and then announced that he'd paid for her meal as well as his own.

'Big spender!' Marcie hissed under her breath.

The driver finished telling a joke to the waitress who laughed loud enough to allow anyone to count all of her teeth; lipstick-smudged ones into the bargain.

'Let's hit the road!' the driver laughed, laying his hand on the waitress's backside with a hearty slap — an action which made her laugh all the more.

Just try that on me, Marcie thought. Just you try!

But what he did was hold the door open for her to step through to where the refuelled Buick was waiting.

* * *

If Marcie's father was silent, her mother was tearful. She didn't sit down and howl; there were no hysterics. What happened was that every so often throughout the day she would realize that she was crying; small, slow tears that drifted from the corners of her eyes and ran down to the corners of her small, tight mouth.

When this happened she would take out a little hand-embroidered handkerchief and dab at her face, until the tears had disappeared — until the next time. The handkerchief had been embroidered by Marcie when she was seven and given to her mother as a Christmas present; her mother had kept it ever since.

She did not like to think of herself as a sentimental woman. Indeed, she thought that anyone who let their feelings get in the way of their good sense was being a fool to themself. But there were always exceptions — and having a daughter run off on you twice, she thought, might well be counted one of those.

By now he had stopped drinking and started swallowing pills. The Buick swerved across the road and only Marcie's alarmed shout and the bright headlights of an oncoming car made the driver pull at the wheel in time.

'What the hell d'you think you're doing?' Marcie shrieked. 'You could have got us killed!'

'No chance, kid. No chance.' He leered over at her. 'Me, I got a charmed life.'

'You must have, to've stayed alive this long.'

'Gonna live forever.'

'Not at this rate, you're not.'

He laughed and swallowed a handful of pills, pink

and orange and yellow. Some sputtered away and bounced along the worn upholstery of the seat. 'Go on,' he urged. 'Take some. Few uppers'll get you through the night just fine. Take enough of them little fellers and if we do run into something you ain't gonna feel a thing!'

He obviously thought he had said something very funny. He slapped his leg, slapped the flat of his hand against the windscreen; he hollered and roared until he broke into a fit of coughing and once more the truck swerved dangerously across on to the opposite side of the highway.

A horn blared, lights flashed and, in desperation, Marcie grabbed at the wheel.

The Buick turned sharply as Marcie fought to bring it back into the right lane. The driver cursed at her, jabbed his foot at the brake and threw his arm out towards her at the same time. His elbow struck Marcie just below the cheekbone and she cried out in pain.

The truck's rear wheels bounced up on to the verge and the driver cursed some more and hauled the wheel round, but too hard. They flew into a skid that turned them through a half circle and threw them off the highway and into the dark. There was a wrenching sound, a high pitched squeal and then a thunderous bang as the side of the truck smashed against a tree.

The driver was hurled forward by the impact and there was a sickening crack as his face and forehead hit the inside of the windscreen. Marcie was tossed to the floor and she lay there, hugging herself as small as she could.

Other vehicles sped by along the highway, east

and west, none stopping. Marcie waited until she was certain that none of her bones was broken and then she pushed herself back up on to the seat. Her right shoulder felt tender and she knew that there was going to be a terrific bruise by morning. The only other place where she was hurting was the left side of her cheek where he had hit her with his elbow.

Marcie sat quite still for several minutes, waiting for her heartbeat and her pulse to calm down. Only then did she take hold of the driver by his shoulders and pull him away from the windscreen. Several rivulets of blood ran over his face in a criss-cross pattern. Over his right eye there was a swelling that was already the size of a small egg and growing all the time. He wasn't dead, Marcie didn't think so, anyway, but he was a dead weight in her hands. She moved them and he fell back against the seat and slowly slumped sideways until the side window prevented him from sliding any further.

The engine had stalled and Marcie reached out and turned off the ignition. She didn't think the whole thing was about to explode but she didn't want to take the chance. She'd taken chances enough for one day.

Her slender fingers reached down into the man's pockets and found his folded stack of dollar bills. Close to one hundred. She took seventy-five for herself, figuring that her needs were greater than his. Then she rooted around under the dashboard until she came up with a torch.

Time to leave.

The ground felt good beneath the thin soles of her sneakers and she ran back on to the highway, lighting her way with the narrow beam of the torch. In less than five minutes she had successfully flagged down a station wagon driven by a Presbyterian preacher who was on his way to visit his maiden aunt in Chicago.

Marcie climbed in, thanked the man in a soft, well-spoken voice, let her head fall sideways against the upholstery and before they'd travelled a mile she was fast asleep.

7

The twin's stepmother had been the first to complain and the last to convince. She thought that what the police lieutenant had suggested was foolhardy and reckless and likely to result in Sam and Lennie getting into serious trouble. 'Who knows what's going to happen to you out there?' she had demanded. 'Running the streets with a bunch of thieves, junkies and perverts!'

'But, Alice,' Sam had protested. 'You can't walk more than half a mile in this city without doing exactly that anyway.'

'Sam's right,' Lennie had chimed in, 'New York's pretty much wall-to-wall sleaze. Every time you listen there are police sirens wailing off, ambulances, all kinds. Look in the paper or turn on the news and there's people getting shot or robbed or both.'

'That doesn't mean you have to go out looking for it,' Alice had replied, alarmed.

'But maybe it does,' Sam had said, with such force that everyone stared at him.

'Explain,' said Howard, after several seconds.

'Well, if the city is as bad as Lennie's claimed, and if the lieutenant's right and there are more and more young kids getting sucked into it, then don't you think the one thing we should do *is* to get more involved?'

'I don't think I understand,' Alice had said.

'I think I'm beginning to,' said Howard, softly.

'Every time I go out in Manhattan,' Sam continued, 'say, somewhere like 42nd Street or Times Square, there are these really smart people, law abiding, lots of money, walking along pretending not to notice the down-and-outs who are begging or just lying in doorways sleeping. I remember once, this man and woman came up the steps from the subway — he was wearing a blue suit that must have cost five hundred dollars at the very least, and she was wearing a fur stole wrapped around the top of a yellow dress that was some kind of shimmery material, all spangled over with sequins. Fifty yards along the pavement, this white kid was stretched out — he couldn't have been much older than Lennie or I — he was sprawled right across the pavement, vomit sticking to his front where it had dried and blood smeared across his face. This couple, they just stepped over him, as if he was a piece of trash, as if he wasn't worth a moment's thought or consideration — as if whatever he was, he wasn't human any more.'

Alice stood there shaking her head. 'That's terrible,' she said.

'What's more terrible,' Sam had gone on, 'is the fact that after calling them all the names I could think of inside my head, I went and did the same thing myself. I just walked on by.'

'But you noticed him,' said Howard. 'You didn't treat him with the same contempt as that couple did.'

'As far as that kid was concerned,' said Sam, 'I might as well have done. The only difference was that I felt sorry for him and angry at the way others were treating him. But I didn't *do* anything about it.'

57

'And now you intend to,' Howard had said, understanding.

'Now Lennie and I have been offered a chance to help,' Sam had replied, 'and I think we should take it.'

'But the danger . . .' Alice interrupted.

'We're not going to be out there on our own,' Lennie had reminded her. 'We'll be part of a police undercover operation. We're not going out there to take on the New York underworld single handed. We're not vigilantes.'

Howard had put his arm around Alice's shoulder and given her a squeeze. 'What the boys are saying makes a lot of sense,' he had told her. 'And there's something else we ought to bear in mind — if Jackie Eves hadn't done what she could for them once or twice we would never, all four of us, be standing here now.'

Alice had nodded glumly. She still didn't like it, but there was no way she could deny the arguments. Sam and Lennie had been asked to help in something important and help was what they ought to do.

'We'll be okay, Alice,' Lennie had assured her. 'You don't have to worry about us.'

'That's right,' Sam had added, giving her the most cheerful smile he could muster. 'We're going to be fine.'

That had been three weeks ago.

Now they were back in Central Park in the middle of a weekday afternoon, the sky was beginning to cloud over and they were getting numb from doing nothing. They were on a grassy knoll near where the zoo was being rebuilt and restructured. Right now there were no animals; instead of bears and giraffes, there were bulldozers and workmen in yellow hard-hats, forever calling out at the passing women and singing at the tops of their voices.

Lennie was wearing an old sweat shirt and frayed jeans with rips at both knees; Sam had on a denim shirt that had been his father's and which was blotched with paint, denim cut-offs and a baseball cap pulled down over his fair hair.

They'd been in that spot for a couple of hours now, waiting for a meeting neither of them thought was going to happen. Not any longer.

They had met Zoe the previous Sunday. She had been wandering through the builders' site that had been the zoo, shaking her head from side to side and pausing every now and then to talk to the animals. Sam and Lennie had watched her from a distance — a fifteen, sixteen year old in a worn-out print dress and soiled sneakers, her hair a tangle of yellow rats' tails, her face scarred and dirty — as she moved round and round where the cages had been, stopping and calling, stopping and calling.

A few passers-by had laughed in her dirty face; most, as usual, looked the other way. After a while, Sam went over and lightly touched her shoulder.

Zoe screamed.

'It's okay,' Sam had said quickly, backing off a little.

Zoe blinked at him, as if trying to get him in focus.

'It's okay,' he said again, gently.

She craned her head towards him, holding it a little to one side.

'The animals,' Sam said, 'they're gone.'

Zoe had looked at him, her lower lip started to tremble, she bit down into it with her front teeth and began to cry.

Five minutes later they were sitting on a bench, the three of them, Sam, Lennie and Zoe. The girl had stopped crying, more or less. Every so often a tear would trickle down on to one cheek or the other, much as water will drip from a leaky tap.

'They've been put down,' she snivelled. 'Shot.'

'No,' Sam had assured her. 'They're in other zoos, waiting to come back here.'

Zoe's dark little eyes looked at him for a moment with bright hope. 'Really?'

Sam nodded. 'Really.'

But the hope faded as quickly as it had arrived. 'No,' she said. 'You're lying to me.'

'I'm not,' said Sam.

'He's not,' said Lennie.

'Yes, he is,' said Zoe. 'He is. Everyone always lies. Always. They're dead. Dead!'

'No . . .' Sam began, but she jumped up from the seat and jabbed an angry finger towards his face.

'Liar!' she had screamed at him. 'Liar!'

The arm whipped back with surprising speed and the bony fist came hard towards his face. Sam caught it, inches away from his cheek, and held it fast. She stood there, glaring down at him, fear and hatred mixed together in her dark eyes. Sam looked into her face and then away at the taut whiteness of her arm — at the tiny but unmistakable scars of needle marks standing out dark against the skin.

Zoe's sudden flash of anger had subsided almost as rapidly as it had flared up. All of her moods were the same. It was impossible to predict how she would be feeling or reacting from one minute to the next. She did calm down enough, though, for the twins to get her to walk out of the zoo with them and sit on a bench

60

and share something to eat. She even talked about where she had come from — a mobile home in New Jersey where she had lived with her stepfather until he had hit her that once too often. After that, like a lot of kids with nowhere else to head for, she had made her way to New York, Manhattan, The Big Apple. About the only good memory she had of her real father was that he had taken her once to the Central Park zoo. It had been one of those days in childhood which seemed to have gone on forever; the sun had always been shining and the sky had stretched over the world in a forever kind of blue. Zoe had held her father's hand and talked to the animals. She had been perfectly, blissfully happy. She had been seven years old.

Now, she sat there like she was sitting on an electric fence, suspecting that at any second some malicious hand would switch on the current.

Sam had tried asking her about the people she'd met since coming to the city, wanting to find out whatever information he could without letting her think that he was prying.

But she was cautious and careful not to say anything specific. She talked of meeting a guy down in Greenwich Village who had let her crash out on his floor for a time; about another guy who had given her ten dollars to buy food, someone else who had paid her to spend the afternoon sorting out magazines into bundles; a woman with a leopard-skin dress who had given her the key to her apartment for a week if Zoe would promise to water her plants and feed her goldfish.

'She just gave it to you?' said Lennie, disbelievingly.

'Sure,' Zoe flashed. 'Why shouldn't she?'

'No reason,' said Lennie hastily back-pedalling.

Zoe made her small hands into fists and pummelled them against her skinny knees. Sam made a signal to Lennie to be cool, but it was too late. The girl jumped to her feet and began to walk away.

'Maybe we could meet up again?' Sam had suggested, going after her.

'What for?'

'No reason. Just to hang out.'

'What d'you want from me?'

'Nothing.'

'Liar! Everybody wants something from me.'

Sam gave her his best smile. 'Maybe we just want to be your friends.'

For a moment, she wavered. Sam could see her wanting to believe him, straining to. But all of the things that had happened to her since the time her father had taken her to see the animals, at seven years old, conspired against her. 'You're a liar!' she screamed into Sam's face. 'You're both liars!'

And she grabbed at the loose skirt of her dress and ran.

'Zoe!' Sam had shouted after her. 'The hill by the entrance. We'll be there. Come see us! Tomorrow!'

They had gone back there the next day, and several days following. There had never been any sign of Zoe.

Zoe at the zoo.

Just like so many of the runaways they had made contact with; all of them afraid and hungry, desperate for any sign of love or friendship and terrified to take it when it appeared. Hiding in corners. Lost and frightened to be found.

Kids talked to them — sometimes — and yet they never said anything that really mattered. They talked in riddles or they left huge gaps in the stories they were telling, gaps which Sam and Lennie could only fill with their imaginations. As for any real leads, anything that would link up these runaway kids with what the police thought was going on in the city's drug trade, there seemed to be nothing. Nothing concrete.

Yet whenever they met up with the lieutenant — always in some undercover meeting place where they could hope to go unnoticed — Jackie Eves seemed pleased enough.

'But we're getting nowhere!' Lennie had complained bitterly.

'How can you say that?' the lieutenant had asked.

'Nobody tells us anything.'

'What do you expect? You're not priests hearing confession.'

'Then how can it help?'

'Everything you pass on to me gets passed on to the officers manning the computer. Each little bit of evidence, every shred of information we get, it might mean nothing alone, but sift it all together and gradually we'll get the wider picture.'

Lennie had frowned. 'Gradually!' he scoffed. 'I've had it with gradually.'

'Look,' Jackie Eves had said, 'this is a big problem. You're not going to solve it yourselves and no one's going to solve it in a day. Understood?'

Lennie had sighed but nodded. Understanding didn't mean that he liked it any the better.

'Keep one thing in mind,' the lieutenant had said at the end of the meeting, 'these kids may not be saying anything much to you, but they're saying a whole lot less to us. You're doing good, don't be to hard on yourselves. Okay?'

Okay or not, Sam and Lennie were there in the park, on the hump of grass, waiting for a terrified shrimp of a girl from New Jersey, with fear in her dark eyes and needle marks on the insides of her arms, to show her face.

And all the while the sky grew darker and the clouds thickened.

'We're going to get soaked,' said Lennie, looking at their skimpy clothes.

'Maybe it'll pass over,' Sam said, optimistically.

'And maybe the sun will suddenly shine and Zoe will come walking over the horizon, ready to lead us to all the bad guys,' suggested Lennie, sarcastically.

At that moment there was a rumble of thunder in the air and soon after that the dark sky above the tall buildings to the west of where they were sitting was lit up by a flash of lightning.

'What do you reckon?' asked Sam, getting rapidly to his feet.

'I reckon we make a run for it,' replied Lennie.

They sprinted for the nearest cover and skidded to a halt beneath the edge of a thick canopy close to where the builders were working. It was yellow tarpaulin and the rain struck it like peas being fired from a rapid-rate peashooter. Rain bounded back from the concrete at their feet, stinging Sam's bare legs and soaking Lennie's jeans. More thunder growled, ominously.

'This could go on for hours,' complained Lennie.

'At least we've got some kind of shelter,' said Sam. 'We could have got stranded in the middle of it.'

Lennie rubbed splashes of water from his body and peered out through the driving lines of rain. Amongst others less fortunate than themselves and scurrying frantically for cover, there was a shape he thought he recognized. 'Hey, look there!'

'Not Zoe?' said Sam, trying to see where his brother was pointing.

'Not exactly,' said Lennie; 'look, running towards the bridge.'

Sam followed Lennie's finger and saw him, a big, bulky figure trundling through the downpour with the speed of a man trying to sprint through water. He was wearing a dark sweater and the side of his hair he had allowed to grow was already plastered to the side of his face, but even so there was no mistaking him.

It was their unfriendly neighbourhood burglar: it was Fat Freddy.

'What d'you think?' asked Lennie.

'I think we go after him,' replied Sam.

Lennie glanced up into the unrelenting rain. 'I was afraid you'd say that,' he grumbled.

The twins left their shelter and chased out into the storm.

8

Whatever Freddy was doing, wherever he was going, there was more to it than simply getting out of the rain. For one thing, he didn't delay under the bridge which carried the motor road over the path. Instead he hurried on as fast as his bulk would permit, doubling back on himself twice before coming out of the park level with East 69th Street.

A line of yellow cabs moved steadily north along Fifth Avenue, rain bouncing from their roofs, tyres swishing arcs of water into the air.

Freddy hesitated on the kerb and then made a dash for it, heading across the street.

The twins hesitated, faces glistening wet, not wanting to get too close and risk being spotted. Not that spotting anyone in this storm was going to be easy. They saw Freddy heading along 69th Street, let him get half the block and then set out after him. By the time they had crossed the avenue he was gone.

'That's not possible,' exclaimed Lennie.

'He's ducked in for shelter,' said Sam.

'What for? He must be soaked to the skin already.'

Sam shrugged and pointed ahead. There was nothing else to do but look. After a few minutes, a sudden flash of lightning made them blink and as their eyes reopened there was the silhouette of Fat

Freddy, poised at the intersection and about to turn left on to Madison Avenue.

'What's he doing that for?' asked Sam, suspicious.

'What?'

'Turning back on himself?'

'Who knows?'

'Then let's find out.'

Their feet splashed along the pavement as they ran into the wind, not wanting to risk losing their man a second time. As they gained the end of the block, they were in time to see him making a left turn, changing direction again and looking as if he were heading east towards Lexington Avenue.

'He acts like a man who doesn't know where he's going,' said Lennie, above the noise of the storm.'You think this rain's got him disorientated or what?'

'Or what,' said Sam.

'Meaning?'

'Meaning, I think he wants to make sure he's not being followed.'

'But he is.'

'I know it. The question is, does he?'

'How do we find that out?'

'We don't. We take this street here, parallel. If we run we should be level with him when he shows at the end of the block, okay?'

There was no time to argue: the twins ran.

And sure enough there was Freddy, pausing to glance over his shoulder but not bothering to look up the street to where Sam and Lennie were peering out.

'Getting careless, Freddy,' said Sam, with a smile.

Freddy carried on his way, changing tack yet again before arriving at the subway station at 68th Street and Lexington.

'If he was heading here all the time,' said Lennie, 'he could have made it in half the time.'

'Which means we were right about him not wanting to be followed.'

'Or being lost.'

'Come off it, Lennie. I've rarely seen a man looking less lost in his life.'

They watched as Freddy slipped his subway token into the barrier and moved on through. The twins had the good sense always to travel with a supply of tokens and so it was easy for them to follow him through.

'Now,' asked Sam out loud, 'uptown or down?'

The answer was uptown. Freddy hesitated before jumping on to the train when it juddered into the station, again as if to make sure no one had the chance to jump on after him. But Lennie managed to wedge a shoulder between the doors, causing them to spring back so that the twins could get on board. They were two cars down from where Freddy had boarded and swiftly they walked between cars, so that they were adjacent to him. From where they were standing, water oozing out of their shoes and dripping from every part of their bodies, they could just see Freddy leaning against the rail near to the doors.

As the train was about to pull out from the 149th Street station, Freddy lunged forward and off on to the platform.

Sam and Lennie were only just quick enough. They jumped off the train and immediately behind a flight of stairs, feeling exposed out there on a mainly empty platform. But Freddy was already marching down in the opposite direction.

'Think he's heading for the street?' asked Lennie.

'No,' said Sam, with a quick shake of the head. 'I think he's changing lines.'

They followed their quarry on to the crosstown train, which took him to 96th Street and Broadway. Still he didn't feel like heading back up to the streets. 'Maybe he's riding the subway till the storm blows itself out?' suggested Lennie.

Sam kept his ideas to himself.

They got on to the A train next, following Freddy back uptown, north towards Harlem. At 168th Street, Freedy shrugged his massive shoulders inside his dark and sodden sweater and took the stairs two at a time, hurrying up back above ground.

'Where are we?'

'Way up above Yankee Stadium. In the Bronx.'

'Where's Freddy?'

'Over the other side of the street. Taking his time.'

It was true. Now that his twisting journey was seemingly through, Fat Freddy didn't seem to have a care in the world — at least not whether he was being followed or not. Plus, he had outridden the storm as well. The sky had all but shed itself of clouds, it was getting lighter and brighter by the minute. There was even a suggestion of sun up there to the west.

The pavements shimmered and steamed as the water began to dry out. Freddy was almost sauntering now, enjoying the fresh air after all that time on graffiti-decorated subway trains. Yes, he was even whistling.

'Hey!' hissed Lennie, 'he's a Motorhead fan.'

Sam raised an eyebrow. 'Nothing could surprise

me less. Why don't the two of you arrange to get together some time — you could swill down can after can of beer and swop notes on heavy metal.'

'You know you're a sarcastic so-and-so, some of the time, Sam.'

Sam grinned. 'And did you know you've just said the most alliterative sentence of your life.'

Lennie wasn't sure what alliterative meant, but he didn't think it was a compliment. 'Are we going to stand here all day listening to you being clever?' he asked.

'It's a possibility,' laughed Sam. 'Alternatively, we could see exactly where our oversized friend is going.'

'Fine,' said Lennie. 'Why don't we do that?'

Fat Freddy was whistling his way towards the Harlem River. He was the perfect picture of a man who didn't have a care in the world; and certainly not the weight of the world on his shoulders (though there was still a lot of weight hanging over the belt of his jeans). He was in such a cheerful mood that as he went diagonally across the street, he switched from Motorhead to Bruce Springsteen. He even tried a little dance step to *Dancing in the Dark*.

'Maybe it's his birthday,' said Lennie.

The twins were watching him from a hundred yards back along the road. To the left side of the road there were tall apartment buildings, mostly with iron grilles across the windows to keep out both the burglars and the pigeons. Opposite, green grass spotted with shrubs and small trees led down to the river.

By now, there was hardly a cloud in the sky and, if it hadn't been for the fact that their shoes still squelched as they walked, Sam and Lennie could have believed that the storm had never happened.

'Whatever was worrying him before,' said Sam, 'it sure has gone with the wind and rain.'

'I guess,' said Lennie, 'that after all that doubling back on his tracks, he's positive no one could still be following him.'

'One thing I'd like to know,' said Sam, 'is why Freddy thought he might be being followed in the first place?'

'Maybe he's on the run from the police,' said Lennie. 'We did catch him red handed about to run off with the petty cash.'

'Not to mention the blueberry pies.'

'I wasn't going to,' said Lennie.

'What?'

'Mention the blueberry pies.'

They looked around at the sound of a car accelerating past them with a squeal of rubber. It was a dark green Buick, a four-door model with smoked-glass windows and white-wall tyres. It swerved around a delivery truck and, with another squeal of the brakes, skidded across the road.

Ahead of them, Freddy stopped in his tracks and turned. He was no longer whistling.

The Buick was headed straight for him.

Sam and Lennie stared, open mouthed.

At the last moment, Freddy turned and tried to run.

The car bumped up on to the kerb, skidded sideways along the pavement, turning sharply so that the rear right side crashed into Freddy and sent him sprawling over the grass.

'Let's go!' said Sam, eagerly.

'Wait!' Lennie grabbed at his arm.

'Come on!' urged Sam.

'What for?'

'They'll kill him!'

Lennie's fingers dug deep into his brother's arm. 'You want them to kill us as well?'

Two men in red bomber jackets had leapt from the back of the Buick. They ran at Freddy and rolled him over fast; one of them hauled him to his knees and the other proceeded to hit him about the head with a tyre iron. The sound of metal smacking against skin and bone echoed through the late afternoon air.

'Let's go!' shouted Sam a second time, and managed to shake himself free of his brother's grasp. He started to sprint across the street, heading for the grass. Lennie watched him go, shook his head in annoyance and then started out after him.

Ahead of them, Freddy was face down on the ground. The length of tyre iron swung high through the air a final time and came down on the back of his skull with a sickening crack.

'Let's go!' called one of the men in bomber jackets, hearing the twins racing towards them. They jumped for the open doors of the car, which throttled away before they were safely inside. There were shouts of alarm mixed with the crashing of gears and the whine of spinning tyres, but finally the two were in the back seat with the doors slammed shut behind them.

Sam stared after the car, trying to identify the number, but the plate had been smeared over with oil or mud and was impossible to read at that speed.

Lennie was kneeling down beside Fat Freddy. His head was at an ugly angle to the rest of his body and blood was slowly spreading from beneath it, mingling with the puddles of water that still had to soak into the earth. Behind his ear, there was a large swelling where the surface of the skin had been torn open.

'Is he still breathing?' asked Sam.

Lennie found his pulse, down along his temple. It was there, but only faintly. 'Just,' said Lennie. 'It's touch and go.'

'Stay with him,' said Sam, moving away. 'I'll phone for an ambulance.'

There was a small tailor's shop on the corner of the block and a stoop-backed old man with a Polish accent and a tape measure hanging from around his neck, allowed him to use the telephone to call emergency. 'Around here,' the old man said, 'it's the only number that gets used.'

Sam gave the details and went back across the street. Lennie was squatting down beside Freddy, who gave no sign of coming round. He still hadn't moved when they heard the wail of the ambulance some minutes later.

The paramedics were young: one was a dark-haired woman whose jaws worked away methodically at a wodge of gum, the other a light-skinned black man with a warm smile. They took one look at Freddy and shook their heads.

'Friend of yours?' the man asked, nodding towards the twins.

'No,' said Lennie.

'We were passing,' said Sam.

'See it happen?' asked the woman through her gum.

'Not really,' said Sam.

'Not much,' said Lennie.

'Tell it to the cops anyway,' said the man. 'Right now, we better get him to emergency before it's too late.'

Gently, but firmly, they turned Fat Freddy over and lifted him on to a stretcher, which they transferred swiftly into the back of the ambulance.

'Must be a knack to it,' commented Lennie, as the ambulance sped away, lights flashing.

'To what?'

'The two of them; they don't weigh any more than us, yet they picked up Freddy like he was no heavier than a couple of cans of beans.'

'It's part of the training,' said Sam.

'I'd like to do that some time,' said Lennie. 'It might be interesting.'

Maybe, Sam thought, though not as interesting as the reasons behind what just happened.

His thoughts were interrupted by the sound of a police car heading down the street towards them. That was followed seconds after by another, coming the wrong way along a one-way street. And then another. 'It's a police convention,' said Lennie.

'Shut up!' said a burly uniformed officer, swinging his truncheon.

Lennie nodded and did as he was told. Sam motioned to him and the two of them started slowly to walk away. They didn't get ten yards before the same officer called after them. 'Back here!'

The twins turned to face him.

'You called this in, huh?'

'Yes,' said Sam.

'Then you stick around and answer questions, right?'

'You told us to shut up,' said Lennie.

'That was then, this is now. Get over here and make a statement. Don't make me have to ask you twice. Understood?'

He tapped his night stick against the palm of his hand to underline the point. Sam and Lennie went back and began to make their statement.

'You know no reason why this guy Freddy might get hit, huh?'

It was fifteen minutes later and every word had been written slowly into the officer's note book.

Sam and Lennie both shook their heads.

'You didn't see the faces of either of the guys that jumped him?'

'Not clearly,' said Sam.

'Not clearly enough to identify them,' said Lennie.

'And you didn't get the number of the car?'

They shook their heads again.

'Great! You been a great help, the pair of you.' He glanced down at his notebook. 'This is your correct address, right? You ain't shooting me a load of bull?'

They assured him that they were not.

'Okay. Get home outta the Bronx, back where you belong. We need to talk to you again, we'll get in touch. And you remember anything, you come up with any bright ideas — not that that looks likely from the pair of you — you get in touch with me, all right? Here's my card. Delaney. That's me. Clear?'

'Clear,' said Sam.

'As crystal,' said Lennie.

Officer Delaney pointed the end of his stick towards Lennie 'You trying to be funny?'

'No, officer,' said Lennie, straight faced.

'Good. Now get outta here.'

The twins didn't need telling twice. They turned and headed back towards the nearest subway station and, as they walked, the wet still squeezed between their toes.

9

It no longer seemed to matter. Marcie's father stood looking at the body of the rooster where it lay in the middle of the yard. The bird's neck was twisted round at an impossible angle from its body, the bright wattle of loose skin hung down from beneath its beak like a piece of Christmas paper that had strayed, forgotten, out into the dirt. The eyes were pin-points, dark and glazed over; the wings folded in at the sides of its brittle body.

Four or five hens pecked around the dead rooster, beaks jerking down at the ground automatically, insensibly.

Marcie's father didn't know who had killed the rooster, how or why. There had been some kind of a kerfuffle in the hen house during the night and most times he would have pulled on his work pants over his long johns, fetched his torch and maybe the old O-O shotgun and gone down to see what all the fuss was about. But last night he had lain there, lumpy mattress pressing against his back in all the wrong places; lain there and stared at the stains on the yellowing ceiling and not moved.

He knew his wife, May, Marcie's mother, was awake beside him; knew that her eyes, also, were open. She had scarcely slept these past two weeks since Marcie had gone. He could hardly sleep himself; kept awake by her lying there, not speaking, not moving, waiting for the birds to start up outside and for the first light to slowly unravel the day. Previously, May had risen at six each morning, winter or summer, fair weather or foul. But now it was five o'clock, now it was four-thirty. And all of this after little or no sleep at all.

So when something, someone, had broken into the yard and disturbed the hens, neither of them had moved or spoken, though both were aware that something was going on.

What did it matter?

What did anything matter?

You raised kids and you worked hard, fed them and clothed them and pushed them off the porch each morning with a lunch box to catch the school bus. You did this and you cuffed them when they went wrong or spoke out of turn. You set them to work hard helping around the place. You made them sit silent once a week when you read them the Bible.

You did what you could.

One by one, you watched them grow up and leave. A son working in the navy yard in San Diego who sent cards at Christmas and New Year, a bunch of flowers on Mothers' Day and a turkey each Thanksgiving. A daughter who married a trucker who drove her down to East Texas and left her there in a four-room frame house with five kids and a back yard crammed with the insides of rusting automobiles. Another son who never could settle more than a couple of months in any one place — they had a football penant from Oklahoma, a stuffed seal from

Anchorage, Alaska, a scribbled postcard from Mexico with no return address.

And now Marcie.

She had run off before, to New York and by good luck and the Good Lord's intervention they had got her back.

Back home and helping her mother with the chores, sitting with them both in front of the TV, snapping open can after can of beer and smoking too many packs of cigarettes; back home and sitting in her room or out on the porch, trying out chords on the guitar her brother gave her the last time he went off, trying out new chords and writing songs.

They had gone into town to see her just the one time, playing with that band in a bar that wasn't fit to keep sheep penned up in. Too many drunks and too much hollering and the women — well, they were a scandal. But Marcie had come up and sang and sounded pretty good. They'd both felt pretty proud and they'd told her so, but they hadn't gone to see her again. Not there — not in a place like that.

It didn't seem right. But then, nothing did: not any more.

Marcie's father turned the dead rooster over with his foot and a small swarm of flies buzzed away from the blood-smeared feathers that were clotted against its chest.

He stood there for some time, shaking his head and from time to time fingering the grey stubble around his chin. Loose skin hung down against his neck in folds like rough sandpaper. The pupils of his eyes were half-covered by a yellow film. Every now and again his foot, as if by some will of its own, tapped impatiently against the ground, yet still he didn't turn away, go back towards the house.

Inside, Marcie's mother was sitting at the kitchen table, every item of cutlery, each knife, fork and spoon that they possessed, spread out on an opened newspaper. The remnants of one of her husband's old work shirts in one hand and a bottle of polish in the other, she was cleaning each piece until she could see her face in the shine.

Last week it had been the plates, the cups and mugs and saucers. The week before that she had taken down every pot and pan and scrubbed it in scalding water. In between, she had taken all the rugs and carpets out of the house, slung them over a line and beat them till the dust hung over the yard like a cloud. She had polished the floors and the furniture and she had wiped away at the glass in all of the windows and washed the woodwork of the frames.

She was working at the house as if she was driven by something she failed to understand.

She did all of this without speaking, without explanation — if her husband had asked her, she would not have been able to tell him why. Not that he did. All that time, those weeks after Marcie left the house, taking her things with her, man and woman, father and mother, scarcely spoke.

Never spoke about Marcie.

Never mentioned her name.

Never had her out of their minds.

Marcie's father walked in through the back porch door and let it swing shut behind him. He went round past the table where his wife was polishing the knives and off into the room at the side of the house where he kept the shotgun, resting on wooden dowels on the wall. He broke it open and slid shells into the twin barrels. There was a bright click as he snapped it shut.

May glanced up from cleaning a silver knife and saw him standing in the doorway, looking down at her. They had had that knife in the family a good many years; it had been given to them the day they were married, a gift from her great aunt Lucie over at Missoula, part of a set that had been given to her on her wedding day. Lord knows how many years that knife has known or seen.

The old man in the doorway still hadn't moved; still stood there with the shotgun resting against the crook .of one folded arm.

May continued to polish the knife. After some more minutes, she set it down, satisfied and, as she did so, her husband walked slowly past her and out through the porch door into the yard.

It no longer seemed to matter.

The hens were still pecking aimlessly around in the dirt and the flies were still swarming around the dead rooster.

Marcie's mother rubbed slowly and carefully at the tines of a silver fork.

The air inside the hen house was oddly sweet and stuffy, warm like the inside of a bed that has lain too long without being turned and laid open.

She gazed at the fork and saw there, for a moment, a man standing young and tall and full of promise, straight-backed and spruce, his fine moustache dark around the edges of his mouth. She looked again and saw herself standing beside him on their wedding day.

She stood up.

She heard the muffled blast of the shot.

The silver spoon slid between her fingers and fell amongst the others, setting up a carillon of sound.

As she set her hand against the porch door, the second barrel of the shotgun was discharged.

She ran.

He was standing in the centre of the hen house, spears of light across his body from the uneven slats of the walls. Feathers floated slowly through the air. She could smell the warmth of fresh blood, see the torn remains of the hens at the corners of her vision. The shotgun stock rested against the floor, tips of the barrels against his leg.

'Come on,' she said, and he jumped, startled.

'Come on inside while I make us some coffee.'

He stared at her through the slanting lines of light and saw a young woman wearing a dress of white, a bouquet of blue and gold flowers resting against her arm, a wedding band, thin and bright and new, shining from her hand.

'Come on inside while I make us some coffee and then you can help me with this letter I have to write. You know you always was the one in the family good with words.'

She held out a hand towards him and he reached forward and held it. The shotgun fell away from his side and struck the ground. Together and still holding hands they walked back into the house.

10

Jackie Eves stared out across the waters of the East River and, as she did so, the first drops of rain began to fall, pitting the grey surface. Over the loudspeakers the Circle Line tour guide was pointing out to a boatload of mostly Japanese and German tourists the sights of the Manhattan skyline. The lieutenant wasn't listening: there were other, more pressing things on her mind. Deep inside the city, behind the fine façade, the drugs war was hotting up. One small gang turned against another. Betrayal was the order of the hour. Crack was the money maker: the drug that was turning over money on the streets, in school playgrounds, the parks and back alleys, the dance clubs and the twenty-four hour cafés.

In the last seventy-two hours five deaths had been reported that were drug related.

A bar had been raided on Second Avenue by a car load of youths wearing Balaclava helmets and wielding baseball bats and an axe. It took ten minutes to turn the place into a shambles and send seven people to hospital, three of them into intensive care.

Late one night, a private party in the expensive and select Tudor City section had been interrupted by gatecrashers who had hauled two of the partygoers out on to the balcony and beaten them within an inch of their lives.

In the early hours of the morning, a patrol car had driven down an alleyway in the East Village and stopped alongside a rubbish bin. Two warring cats had jumped away from it, taking the lid with them and leaving an arm poking out. The boy who had been stuffed down inside was still breathing, despite a knife wound between his shoulder blades and another in his thigh. He was thirteen years old.

There was a war going on out there and the police were losing it.

'I've seen you looking happier,' said Sam, accompanying Lennie back to where the lieutenant was sitting.

The twins had been down below decks to fetch hot dogs with mustard and some Cokes.

'I've been happier,' Jackie Eves agreed. 'A lot happier.'

'I don't imagine it's just the rain making you miserable,' said Lennie.

The lieutenant grinned grimly and shook her head.

'I thought the information was helping,' Lennie pressed her. 'You spoke of building up an overall picture, piecing things together.'

'So we are. But it's slow. Like some gigantic jigsaw.' She took a swig at her Coke. 'I'm just worried that by the time we get everything in place, there are going to be so many dead kids out there, dead or badly injured, the whole of Manhattan will be like a graveyard.'

The twins looked at one another and couldn't think of anything to say. For a while they sat alongside the lieutenant and ate their hot dogs, concentrating on not letting the mustard drip down on to their jeans.

Finally, Jackie Eves screwed up the paper serviette that had held the hot dog, swallowed the remains of her Coke, pushed the serviette down into the paper cup, set the cup between her sneakered feet and looked at Sam and Lennie. 'Tell me about Fat Freddy,' she said.

'We already did,' replied the twins, in unison.

'So tell me again.'

They went through it all from the first time they had encountered Freddy inside the restaurant to the final moments out by the Harlem River. They included everything about the kid with the blueberry pies and threw in the stuff about the strange girl called Zoe they had met talking to the absent animals inside the empty zoo.

Jackie Eves listened and nodded. For some minutes after the twins had finished she didn't say anything, but stared out over the river. 'Look,' she said, eventually, 'I think Freddy may be the key.'

She sounded suddenly so definite, that both Sam and Lennie felt their pulses quicken. They stared at her inquisitively.

'I pulled his sheet back at the station. When you got him busted for breaking into Alice's place, someone got a hot-shot lawyer down to the court with bail money hot in his sticky hand. Three minutes up in front of that judge and he was walking.

'I asked a few questions about the lawyer. His name is Greenglass and he's got an office on Madison Avenue. What he pays for that in a month would pay my rental for the whole year. Interesting?'

Sam nodded. 'Where would Freddy find the money to hire a lawyer like that to represent him?'

'And where,' said Lennie, 'would he find someone ready to pay his bail?'

Jackie Eves gave a quick smile. 'Good questions. The same ones I asked. Only you're asking me and I asked the computer.'

'How did it score on answers?' asked Lennie.

'At first, not so hot, but after I figured out the ways to ask the questions, it got better. Greenglass usually handles people who've burned their fingers in the money market and taken too many short cuts; publishers who are having contractual problems with their authors; occasionally a very expensive divorce case, but only where the parties concerned live in a penthouse suite overlooking Park Avenue.

'Except . . .' Jackie Eves weighed the word on her tongue, enjoying it, beginning to smile again; 'except two years or so back he defended a man named Michael Angelo . . .'

'The painter?' Lennie interrupted.

'Stupid!' said Sam, elbowing his brother hard.

'This Michael Angelo,' the lieutenant went on, 'is more of a gangster. Long shiny limousines, long dark Havana cigars, sleek suits in expensive material, and beautiful women hanging from his arm and never opening their mouths to say a word. He's got no record, everything about him is rumour. But the rumours would fill a fat book.'

'What kind of rumours?' asked Sam.

'Like the rumour that he's connected with the Mafia, not only here in the States, but back home in Sicily. Like the rumour that he once bribed a world heavyweight champion to take a dive in the third round of a big fight; the rumour that he helped some union officials to steal close to three million dollars from their own funds; the rumour that he once controlled between one third and one half of the trade in heavy drugs right here . . .' Jackie Eves swept a hand towards the skyscrapers they were passing. '. . . in the city.'

Sam's eyes shone with the beginnings of real excitement. 'You said *once,* he once controlled all of this.'

Jackie Eves nodded.

'Meaning he doesn't any longer,' said Lennie.

'Meaning that his trade has been pulled out from under his feet by these smaller gangs selling crack,' said Sam.

'Hey, guys!' said the lieutenant. 'Don't get in such a sweat about it, you'll have the whole boat listening to us instead of the loudspeakers.'

'Sorry,' said the twins.

'But you're on the right track,' said the lieutenant.

'And you think that what happened to Freddy fits in with this somehow?' asked Sam.

'I think it's possible. It's a long shot, but as a gamble it's worth staking a little time on. More than any other ideas I've seen around.'

'So you think Freddy was connected with this Michael Angelo?' said Lennie.

'Someone with a lot of money and influence sent Greenglass down to get him out. Someone who wanted to keep Freddy out on the streets. Now that doesn't *have* to be Angelo, but it's a chance. There *is* a connection.'

'And the guys who jumped Freddy and beat him up?' asked Lennie.

Jackie Eves shrugged. 'No positive clues, except

that the way they went about it is similar to the way some of these crack gangs have been operating.'

'Hold on,' said Sam. 'Let me see if I can pull all this together. One: Michael Angelo loses control of the drug trade and wants to get it back. Two: he hires someone who's young enough and street-wise enough to find out what the gangs are doing and where they're operating from. Three: Freddy is the person he hires and it's because he knows he's mixed up in something really dangerous that he thinks he might be being followed around the city.'

'And four,' said Lennie, interrupting, 'when Freddy drops his guard and thinks he's home free, one of the gangs hits him hard.'

The twins sat back and watched the lietutenant's face — from her expression it was clear they'd got it pretty much right.

'Can I ask a question now?' said Sam, a few minutes later.

'Sure.'

'We've just constructed a great theory. Is there any way we can prove any of it?'

Jackie Eves rested her chin against her hands. 'Difficult — we can't go waltzing in on Angelo, he's too careful and besides he's guarded better than the Crown Jewels over in your country. And we can't ask Freddy because . . . well, because our friend Freddy still hasn't recovered consciousness.'

The twins' faces looked glum.

'Hey, guys!' said the lieutenant. 'There's a light at the end of the tunnel. We just can't see it yet, that's all. But at least now we know which direction to look in.'

'So what can be done?' asked Sam, wanting to be convinced.

'Several things. I've got people going over Angelo's business dealings, accounts, tax declarations; see if there isn't something his accountants have missed that we can't haul him in on. I've also got him under twenty-four hour surveillance, phone tap, the whole works. That's for starters.'

'What's the main course?' said Lennie.

'We got a number on the menu,' said the lieutenant. 'I'm not sure yet which one is going to prove the tastiest. But we're checking out the area Freddy was walking in, trying to see where he might have been heading. We're also talking again to everyone who's been involved in gang violence. Even though you didn't get a good look at Freddy's attackers or the Buick they were using, we might come up with something. And then there's what the pair of you are going to turn up, hitting the bus stations and the parks and wherever, asking around for anything anyone can tell you about Freddy's movements in the last week. You'll hear things we wouldn't. Before you didn't know exactly what you were after, now you do. I know you're going to come up lucky.'

'I hope so,' said Sam.

'I know so,' said Lennie, grinning.

'Fine,' said the lieutenant. 'Now what say we relax and enjoy the rest of the tour?'

When the twins got back to Alice's, they were hungry enough to eat king-sized burgers and double portions of French fries; just the smell of walking into the restaurant was enough to make their mouths water. Alice was serving at the ice-cream counter and they went over to ask her if it was okay to go back into the kitchen and help themselves.

'Sure,' she said with a broad smile. 'Oh, and Sam, there's a letter for you. I left it over by the cash register.'

Sam looked at his brother, questioningly.

'Go see who it's from,' said Lennie. 'I'll get the food.'

Sam shrugged and walked over to the cash desk. The envelope was leaning against the register, slim and brown. He picked it up and looked at the writing. He had thought it might have been from his mother in England, but instead of her clear, professional handwriting, this was spidery and uncertain. And the postmark showed that it had been mailed two days before in Great Falls, Montana.

Great Falls.

There was only one person Sam knew who lived there and that was Marcie.

He pushed the envelope down into his jeans pocket and went up to the quiet of his room to read its contents.

11

Dear Sam,

I hope you will forgive me for writing to you like this, right out of the blue. Most specially, as Pa and me never thanked you for what you did for our girl, Marcie, back there in New York City. Put it down to us being so relieved to have our little girl back that we just weren't thinking right.

We figured we had lost her for good, I guess, and having her back to us again — well, it was pretty much like she'd come back from the dead. In a manner of speaking.

But Pa tells me I'm rattling on.

The point of my writing is this. Our Marcie has run off again. Just up and stuffed her things into a big bag and hit out for the highway. Things was getting on top of her out here. She'd been singing with this bunch of musicians, even writing some of her own songs and getting to sing those as well, but I guess it never worked out the way she wanted it.

Seems life has been that way for Marcie, pretty much.

We heard tell of a truck driver Pa knows seeing someone looked a lot like our girl thumbing rides out east on Highway 18. Course we ain't got an idea where she's headed — don't have no way of knowing if she knows herself — but since it was where she went before, it did seem to Pa and me that she might be fixing to get herself back to New York.

Marcie wasn't the kind of a girl as talks to her folks a whole lot — tell the truth none of us in this family goes in for a lot of sitting around jawing — but time to time she did speak of you, son, and the way she spoke I'd say she had more regard for you than most people she knows.

We ain't asking you to go out of your way and try and find her, nor nothing like that. Just that if our girl should stop by to see you, maybe you'd be as kind as to ask her to drop us a line, let us know she's safe. Happy might just be too much to ask.

God bless you, son.

May Tallent

Sam read the letter once quickly, twice more slowly, till he could hear the woman's voice inside his head, even though he had never met her. He was intrigued by the fact that Marcie had been working with a band, had no idea that she could either make up songs or sing them. But his overwhelming feelings were of worry and regret.

When he had talked Marcie out of taking her own life, it was as if, somehow, he had taken on some responsibility for her. For her life. He knew that didn't make any kind of sense, not if you looked at it logically. But common sense and logic didn't have much to do with the way you felt.

He remembered thinking, when Marcie went back on the bus with her parents — all that way across America to the far west — that he couldn't see Marcie settling down happily back in the very life she'd run away from.

After some time had passed, though, he had stopped worrying about her; stopped thinking about her altogether, aside from the odd moment when some memory of her had managed to sneak into his mind. It was easy enough to forget without something there close by to jog your thoughts.

But then there had been the time he had been sitting reading his book and suddenly, instead of the words on the page, it had been Marcie's face looking up at him — the short, rough-cut tawny hair, the brightness of those green eyes.

Sam struggled now to conjure back that vision of her: her eyes; their expression.

As though she had been wanting to tell him something — no, not tell him, ask him. Ask him for what? Advice? Help?

'We ain't asking you to go out of your way and try and find her, nor nothing like that.'

Sam set aside the letter and walked across the room to the small chest of drawers in which he kept some of his things. Underneath a pile of T-shirts and an old grey sweater he never wore he found a large brown envelope and pulled it out.

Inside were a letter from his mother, the first she had written to Lennie and himself when they had moved across the Atlantic to live with Howard and Alice. There was his school report, the last from his primary school, the one with all the excellents and hard-workings; a photograph of his grandparents, taken in their garden in Yorkshire, the garden where he and Lennie had spent so much time playing as kids; a picture of Howard and his mother sitting together at a small table outside a café, somewhere on holiday, somewhere in Europe, some time before the twins had been born.

And there was a picture postcard, postmarked Great Falls.

The words on the back: 'This is where I am. Look hard and you'll see me.'

Sam heard footsteps outside and quickly slid the card and the other things back inside the envelope; slipped the envelope out of sight. As Lennie came into the room, Sam was turning, pushing the drawer shut behind his back.

'What's up?' Lennie asked, bouncing towards Sam.

'Nothing.' Sam shrugged, turning away.

'Something's got to be.'

'Why?'

'For one thing, I've been sitting downstairs for ages watching your burger grow cold on the plate. I ate the fries.'

'Good for you.'

'Alice says she'll reheat the burger.'

'Tell her not to bother.'

'God! Something has got into you, hasn't it?'

'No!' Sam snapped.

'You don't have to bite my head off.'

'Lennie, why don't you go back downstairs and leave me alone?'

'Because.'

'Because what?'

'I want to know what's going on.'

Sam sighed. 'Suppose it isn't any of your business?'

'Since when?'

'Since when what?'

'Did you have business that wasn't mine, too – that was secret?'

'Maybe since now.'

Lennie pushed his hands down into his jeans pockets. 'Is it Mum?'

'No.'

'The letter, was it from her?'

'No.'

'About her?'

'Lennie!'

'I was worried, okay? I thought . . .' Lennie stopped and pulled his hands back out of his pockets, then hooked his thumbs down over his belt.

'Look, it's nothing to do with Mum. It's not family stuff. It's just . . . it's personal, that's all. All right?'

'You're not going to tell me about it?'

Sam hesitated no more than a moment. 'No, I don't think so. Not now. No.'

Lennie's gaze shifted over to where the letter was lying, on top of the table in the centre of the room. Sam followed his stare, walked across and folded it back into its envelope and pushed that down into the back pocket of his jeans.

'Lennie . . .'

'Yes?'

'I'm going for a walk.'

Lennie shrugged and stood aside. Only when his brother had stepped through the door did he say, 'You want me to come with you?'

Sam didn't answer: he just kept on walking.

From the centre of Brooklyn Bridge, you could look back over the heart of the city and see a thousand lights, imagine a million lives, people together, people lost and alone.

Sam stood there for a long time, his body leaning forward against the ironwork of the bridge, the traffic moving back and forth behind him in a constant stream. It was cold, up there exposed to the wind that rose off the river, but if he noticed Sam gave no sign. He continued to stand there, staring out, staring, as if looking for something it was impossible to see.

'This is where I am. Look hard and you'll see me.'

12

Marcie woke to such a vast and bright night sky that for several seconds she thought she was back in Montana. The hardness of the step on which she was stretched soon made her realize that was not the case. What she was looking up at was a huge constellation painted across the curved roof of the concourse — she was at the centre of the Grand Central Terminal, one of the two main New York stations. By day, there was the constant hum of passengers, hurrying to get their tickets and bustle off to the fifty or so tracks where trains would be waiting. By night, it was a warm haven for scores of people with no room, no bed, other than what they could scrounge. They slept in the corners, on and underneath the benches, or like Marcie on the wide marble stairs leading down to the concourse floor.

She shifted her legs gingerly, aware that her muscles were beginning to tighten painfully with cramp. Several layers of newspaper were wrapped around the lower part of her body; her scuffed and worn leather jacket was zipped up to her neck, hands pushed into its sleeves.

The hands of the world's largest indoor clock told her that it was eleven minutes past three in the morning.

Marcie shivered.

She turned her head and looked at the shaggy dark hair of the black man sleeping on the step above her. His mouth was open and he was snoring deeply, a resonant satisfied sound. Below her a woman with a grey face, layers of dirt grimed into its crevices, shifted endlessly, moaning lightly as she pushed her arms and legs against the inside of the cardboard carton that served as her sleeping bag.

Down towards the centre of the concourse, close to the information desks, a drunk in a dinner jacket was sitting cross-legged, playing patience with a deck of cards. Each time the card he wanted turned up he would laugh and clap his hands and from all around the sides of the building, voices would call back at him, warning him to be quiet and let folks sleep.

Marcie slid her legs out of the newspaper and sat for a while with her knees hugged inside her folded arms.

That wasn't any good: all it did was make her think of home.

All home did was remind her that she was cold and hungry.

She stood up and stepped carefully over the grey-faced woman, tiptoeing down to the floor; walking diagonally across it, keeping her feet as quiet as she could.

The drunk clapped his hands again and someone threw an old shoe at him from one of the corners. The drunk clambered to his feet, picked up the shoe and, with a thankful smile on his lopsided face, tried to fit it over one of the shiny black shoes already on his feet.

Marcie went up the stairs and pushed her way through the heavy glass doors, out on to 42nd Street.

* * *

She saw the kid before he saw her, and dropped back into the shadows. He was a scrawny little thing, looked as if a good wind would blow him not just over but inside out. He was making his way down the street, shoulders hunched, trying to make out he was strolling through the night without any special idea of where he was going or why.

But Marcie knew better. Marcie remembered.

When she had lived in the city before, there had been nights when she had done the same things. That had been when she had hung out with a bunch of pickpockets and petty thieves — kids she had figured were her friends, until it had all started to go very wrong and she'd learned differently.

That had been when she had met Sam Tempest. Sam . . .

Marcie dug her fingernails hard into the palms of her hands; she didn't want to think about him either, no more than she wanted to think about home. Instead she made herself concentrate on the skinny kid. Watched him as he lifted a loaf of rye bread from the long boxes that had been delivered to the rear door of the bakers, as he took a pint of milk from outside one café, a couple of danish pastries and a yogurt from outside another. His thin fingers moved fast as he passed a twenty-four hour grocer's, lifting two apples, a bunch of bananas and a pineapple and pushing them down skilfully into the front of his loose jacket.

Marcie, keeping tabs from a safe distance, was impressed. She couldn't have done it better herself — which was why she was happy to let him do the job for her.

When she came to the next intersection, she ran left and then right, keeping to her quiet toes, getting ahead of the kid instead of behind him. She had seen enough.

The first thing the kid saw was a sudden movement in front of him, too fast for him to know what — or who — had caused it. His mouth was open to shout, but the sound had only broken from his lips when the outside of a small, hard hand struck sideways against his adam's apple.

The would-be shout became a wordless gurgle.

The gurgle became a harsh choking sound as the same fingers that had hit him closed tight and fast around his windpipe.

The kid's eyes bulged, staring into the face of his attacker and he realized with surprise and shame that it was a girl.

A girl!

Her green eyes glared a warning and the fingers tightened still further. He thought she meant to choke him to death there and then, but instead she set the index finger of her other hand against his lips, signalling for him to be silent.

He nodded agreement as best as he could and she slowly loosened her grip until he was able to gulp in air like a man saved from drowning. Of course, this made him choke and splutter and the only way the girl could get him to stop was to pat him abruptly in the middle of his back.

She patted him so hard she almost knocked him into the wall.

'Come on,' she said, gesturing towards a narrow alley that led off between two nearby buildings.

A couple of cats stopped hissing at each other and raced off along the tops of a line of garbage cans.

100

The girl leaned back against the graffiti-strewn brickwork and stared at him. She doubted if he was much more than fourteen and he weighed about as much as the average ten year old.

'You're too skinny to be eating all that food you just stole,' she said.

'I didn't . . .' he began.

'Don't lie to me, kid,' she said. 'I saw you.'

'How?'

'I followed you.'

'You couldn't have. I'd have seen you.'

Marcie smiled. 'But you didn't. And I can give you a full inventory of what's stashed away under that jacket of yours. All of which amounts to far too much for you to eat all by yourself.'

'It ain't all for me,' said the boy.

'That's right! Half's for me.'

'That's what you think!' said the kid, getting some of his spirit back.

Marcie pushed herself off the wall. 'Kid, it's what I know.'

'If I don't get back with this, I'm for it.'

'You don't hand over half and you're for it.'

'I can't do that.'

'Better to leave with half than have me take the whole lot.'

'You and who else!'

Marcie laughed in his face. Just because the pain was fading from where she had hit him, all of his street courage was returning. Well, let him try if he was foolish enough.

He was and he did.

Marcie watched him feint as if to go further along the alley, then duck low and turn, starting to sprint towards the street. She watched, still smiling, hardly seeming to move. Her left leg snaked out, and curled around the kid's ankle, bringing him crashing to the dirty ground.

One side of his face grazed on the rough concrete and the skin was shredded from the knuckles of his right hand. He was still in that position when Marcie landed on top of him, her knee thumping down into the small of his back, smack between his kidneys.

His mouth opened wide as all the breath was driven out of him. Fingers grabbed at the back of his hair and yanked his head backwards.

'Hey!' he shouted.

'Hey, what?'

'Hey, let go!'

Marcie slammed his face forwards against the ground and held it there. 'You want to eat dirt or you want to eat what you've got mashed up inside that jacket — half of it?'

He mumbled something she took as 'half of it', and she leaned back off him; turned so that she was standing over his skinny body, straddling him.

'Turn round!' she ordered.

He did as he was told. There was blood on the side of his face and trickling from one nostril and there were tears in his eyes.

'What's the matter?' she asked.

'Girls aren't supposed to be able to do stuff like that.'

Marcie threw back her head and laughed. 'What's your name, kid?' she said, when she was through laughing.

'Neb.'

'What kind of a name is that?'

'It's what I get called.'

'Fine,' she agreed. 'Neb it is.' She shook her head and held out a hand to haul him to his feet. 'Hi!' she said. 'I'm Marcie. Now why don't you get that stuff out where we can both see it and get it divided up — all of this exercise is making me hungry.'

She found out that Neb was squatting in an apartment building that was due to be pulled down and replaced by a glass tower of offices. Until then Neb and his friends were sharing it with a floating population of winos and rats. There were three of them, apparently — Neb himself, a Puerto Rican fifteen year old called Luis, and a Vietnamese they called Charlie, although that wasn't his right name.

'Regular United Nations, huh?'

'We get along.'

'But they send you out to steal the food?'

'That's okay,' Neb shrugged. 'They do other things.'

Marcie knew from her own experience some of the ways kids hustled to make a living on the New York streets, so she didn't ask questions, simply nodded. 'And you make out okay, huh?' she said, after a while.

'It was better when Freddy was there.'

'Freddy?'

'Sure. He was older. He had connections. He was into some real tough operations.' Neb stopped, seeing the smile of disbelief spreading across Marcie's face. 'You don't have to believe it, but it's true. Freddy was smart. He made real money. Like I said, he had connections. Big connections.' Neb lowered his voice. 'He was in with the mob.'

'The mob?' repeated Marcie.

'You heard me.'

'You mean, *the* mob? The Mafia.'

Neb's eyes were bright. 'Sure.'

Marcie shook her head. 'Kid, you've seen too many gangster movies.'

'It's true. There was this guy, Freddy did favours for him.'

'Yeah? And lived in some crummy apartment building ready to be demolished. What kind of favours were these? He cleaned some big shot's shoes once in a blue moon?'

'Funny!'

'I thought so.'

'Freddy lived there on account of it was good cover. Anyway, there's a lot of drug pushing goes on around there.'

'That's what your friend Freddy was doing for the mob, pushing drugs?'

'No.'

'Then what?'

'You ask too many questions.'

Marcie jerked a finger towards the end of the alley. 'Come on, kid . . .'

'Quit calling me kid!'

'Okay, Neb. Come on, let's go ask your pal Freddy questions instead.'

'Why?'

'On account it sounds pretty interesting. Besides, I'm between jobs right now — he might think of something I could do to raise a little cash.'

'No chance,' Neb said.

'How come?'

'You can't even ask Freddy no questions, not now. Can't see him.'

'You're going to stop me?'

Neb shook his head. 'He ain't talked to no one in days.'

'Maybe he'll talk to me,' said Marcie.

'If he does, it'll be a miracle. He's in the hospital, intensive care. He got beat up pretty bad. We tried to get to see him but there was this cop sitting outside his room.'

Marcie looked at Neb, thoughtfully. 'Too bad,' she said. 'But let's go see Luis and Charlie anyway. They must be getting pretty hungry by now, waiting for breakfast.'

13

Sam went through the next couple of days like a grizzly bear that had trodden on a thorn and with each fresh step pushed it deeper into its foot. All of the others — Lennie, Alice, Howard, Ruth — quickly learned that it was best to steer clear of him and say as little to him as possible. Sam ate alone, when he ate at all, and wherever his mind was, it certainly wasn't there in the restaurant.

'There was a message from the lieutenant,' Lennie said to him one morning. 'She wants to meet us. Says it's urgent.'

Sam didn't even bother to look up. 'You go.'

'Maybe you didn't hear what I said . . .'

'I heard.'

'She said "urgent".'

'I know.'

'She also said "us". She wants to meet us. US. Watch my lips.'

Sam's hands moved with more speed than Lennie was prepared for. They grabbed him by the front of his sweat shirt and held him fast, their faces close together.

'You're the one who didn't hear me,' Sam said, tight-lipped. '*You* go.'

Lennie shrugged and looked away; Sam let him go.

'What shall I tell the lieutenant?'

'What you like!'

Lennie turned away, shaking. He'd never known his brother like this. After all, he, Lennie, was the one who had moods, he was the one who was up one moment and down the next; he had always been the unpredictable one. Not Sam.

Sam was straightforward; Sam was dependable.

Sam, according to grown-ups, had always been the more grown-up of the two. He was the intelligent one, the boy who did well at school in the classroom as well as on the sports field; he was the one whose hand always went up first in answer to any serious question. It was Sam who read the longest books in the shortest space of time. Sam who, some day, would go waltzing off to university and come back years later with glasses, a slightly stooped back and a carrier bag crammed with degrees. You knew where you were with Sam.

Well, maybe that had been true in the past, but now . . .

'How's Sam?' Ruth asked, when Lennie passed her on the stairs.

Actually she shouted as she had the volume of her personal stereo turned up to full and was blasting the inside of her head with Bananarama.

'Still the same,' Lennie shouted back and Ruth nodded, popping a bubble of bright pink gum back over her lips.

'How's Sam?' Alice asked.

She was stirring something rich and luscious inside a wide mixing bowl.

'Don't ask me,' said Lennie, using a finger to scoop some of the mixture away from the bowl's edge.

'Don't do that!' said Alice, sharply, aiming the wooden spoon at his hand and missing. 'And I already did; ask, I mean.'

'He's still not worth talking to,' said Lennie, backing away. 'And I think that needs a little more sugar.'

'Nobody asked you that,' said Alice.

'Sorry.'

'What is your brother doing, if he's not talking?'

'Pretending to read.'

'Pretending?'

'Unless he's developing a technique which involves reading the words upside down.'

Alice glanced at Lennie and sighed. 'Do you think we should send for the doctor?'

'No, he'll snap out of it.'

'When?'

'When he's good and ready.'

'You're a great help, Lennie.'

'Thanks. And don't forget the sugar.'

Alice aimed the spoon towards his head, so Lennie grinned and got out of the kitchen. He was almost in time to collide with his father, who was wandering aimlessly through the restaurant, whistling.

It always surprised Lennie that his father, who spent quite a lot of his time composing background music for films, whistled off-key and out of tune. But then, having heard some of his music . . .

'How's Sam?' asked Howard, coming to an abrupt halt, his nose almost closer to Lennie's than his own.

'Why don't you ask him?'

'I tried.'

'And?'

'He all but snapped my head off.'

'He tried shaking mine off.'

'It's nothing to do with your mother, you're sure of that?'

'Sure.'

'Well, something's eating him.'

'Perhaps it's a tape worm.'

'Lennie . . .'

'Or some kind of virus — one of those really virulent ones that can take over your whole body from the inside.'

'Lennie . . .'

'Maybe even at this very moment, it's multiplying inside him, each tiny head turning into a hundred others; till this gigantic hydra-headed parasite will start working its jaws off inside Sam's organs, gobbling him up by the greedy mouthful.'

'Lennie! Lennie, you're going too far!'

'No, I'm not, Dad. Just off to meet the lieutenant, down at Battery Park. I'll be back for lunch. Bye!'

So Ruth continued to put her inner ear under too much stress as she exercised her jaws on strawberry-flavoured spearmint; Alice decided that Lennie was right and added sugar to the cake mix, which she carried on mixing; Howard found a piece of manuscript paper in his back pocket and wrote down the tune he'd been whistling before he forgot it; Lennie walked through the financial district for his meeting with Lieutenant Jackie Eves, currently working undercover for the New York Police Department; and it was Karen — back from taking photographs of flowers and shrubs in Maine to work in the restaurant — who finally got Sam to talk.

But that was later.

Jackie Eves was sitting on a bench, wearing a red and green checked shirt, beige chinos, red and white basketball boots and with a small leather bag hanging from one shoulder. The bag contained thiry-two dollars and some change, a set of keys, a small jar of banana and coconut lip balm and a .38 calibre Colt revolver. Jackie Eves was leaning back in the sunshine, enjoying both the weather and what remained of the large pretzel she was eating, complete with mustard.

'How's it going?' she said, as Lennie slipped on to the bench alongside her.

She hadn't seemed to have turned her head in any way, nor given any other sign that she had seen Lennie approaching, but there was no doubt that the lieutenant could see everything and everyone she was interested in.

'Where's Sam?' Jackie Eves asked, a few moments later.

'He's got things on his mind,' said Lennie.

'Uh-huh. Us, too; see that guy over there, the one selling pretzels?'

Lennie looked over to where a large black man, wearing a bright red and yellow beret, was standing behind his pretzel cart, dispensing food to the six-deep queue who were waiting fairly patiently for the ferry that would take them out to the Statue of Liberty.

'What about him?'

'I think he's selling more than pretzels.'

'Drugs?'

'It's sure not extra mustard.'

They sat there for a while, watching to see if the lieutenant was right, but nothing out of the ordinary seemed to be happening.

'Is this what you wanted to see us about?' Lennie asked.

'Not exactly. This is part of it, though. We picked up a kid last night over in the East Village. Tried mugging what he figured was a helpless old woman, but, unfortunately for him, she was an undercover decoy with a black belt in karate. Broke the kid's arm like it was a twig.

'When they got him back to the station, he had marks on his arms from where he'd been injecting himself with heroin. Wasn't any more than fifteen. Come up from Texas six months back. Ran off on his birthday, leaving the candles waiting to be blown out on the cake. He's been using, and selling a little, too. We asked him some names, showed him some pictures, the only one he recognized was a Vietnamese kid he called Charlie. Mean anything to you?'

Lennie shook his head.

Jackie Eves grinned. 'Sit tight.'

The queue for the ferry grew longer and longer and out there at the opening of the East River the newly repainted lady of the Statue of Liberty held her torch high and waited to greet them when they eventually landed. Two buskers were working the queue, a harmonica player who sang and accompanied himself on a selection of old soul songs of the sixties and a juggler who was working himself up to keeping three apples, two oranges and one baseball in the air at the same time.

The queue shuffled, tossed down money into the buskers' hats, ate their pretzels and watched as the next ferry moved with worrying slowness across the water towards them. Off to the left, a battered-looking van slowed to a halt.

Instantly, Jackie Eves was on the alert.

Sensing the change in the lieutenant, Lennie tensed and looked around.

'Watch!' Jackie Eves hissed. 'I'm not sure what's going to go down, but whatever does, you keep your eyes on the delivery boy. When he takes off, follow him. Whatever you do, don't get too close; on no account try and stop him. What we want to know is where he runs to. Got it?'

Lennie nodded. He had it clear. He watched as a slim oriental boy jumped from the front of the van, hurried to the rear and opened it up. He slid out first one, then a second tray of fresh salted pretzels and balanced them on one knee while he slammed the door shut.

'That's Charlie?' asked Lennie, watching the boy approach the queue.

'That's him.'

After that there was no time for talk.

The Vietnamese delivery boy went cheerily up to the pretzel seller, who pulled open the side of his cart, in order to slide the fresh delivery into place.

They exchanged a few words and then, instead of turning swiftly away with his empty trays, the boy reached into an inside pocket and, for a moment, a white envelope showed clearly as it changed hands. The seller pushed the envelope inside his overall and passed over a tight roll of dollar bills in return.

It was what the lieutenant had been waiting for. She sprang from the bench with the speed of an Olympic sprinter taking off from the blocks and headed for the pretzel cart fast.

There was a warning shout from Charlie, who was looking in the lieutenant's direction, and the seller swung round in alarm. He grabbed hold of the cart and pushed it as hard as he could towards the sprinting policewoman. A second later, he barged his way through the edge of the queue and began to run himself.

Jackie Eves jumped wide of the flying cart and changed direction without losing speed.

The seller found himself running right at one of the buskers who astonished him (to say nothing of the audience in the queue) by dropping his oranges, apples and baseball and suddenly juggling a police special into his hands in their place.

The seller skidded sideways and tried to burst through the crowd. His right foot squelched down on to one of the discarded oranges and he began to slide. People jumped out of his path and screamed. The pretzel seller rolled, his bright beret falling from his head as he went. By the time he stopped rolling, less than a couple of minutes later, Jackie Eves was standing over him with her .38 in her hand, and was starting to read him his rights. The undercover juggler reached inside his overalls and removed the envelope, containing several hundred dollars' worth of illegal drugs.

Lennie, from his position on the bench, was watching none of this. Instead, he watched the Vietnamese boy as he wove his way through the massed lines of the queue, heading back towards the van until he realized that the harmonica player was another undercover cop and his retreat was already covered.

He turned on his heels and squeezed between the people who were watching excitedly as the pretzel seller was chased and arrested. For some moments Lennie lost sight of him, only to pick him out a hundred metres further along, ducking through the edge of the crowd, under the barrier and starting to walk, as innocently as he could, through Battery Park in the direction of the US Custom House.

Lennie jumped down from the bench and set off in pursuit.

14

The building was boarded up. Red and black graffiti adorned the walls, and most of the garbage sacks that had been littered outside had been torn into by cats or rats or worse. The temperature was high enough for the stench to hit home from across the street.

Across the street was precisely where Lennie was crouching. He had successfully followed the fleeing Vietnamese boy through the city and now he bent low in the doorway of a hardware store and watched as Charlie clambered over the rotting sacks of refuse and struggled to reach the back window that was no more than an inch open.

His fingers pushed the frame higher and his arms disappeared inside as he grasped the inside sill and pulled himself up. Another few seconds and his legs wriggled through and out of sight.

Lennie was already on his way across the street.

Lennie peered through the gap at the bottom of the window and found himself looking into a dimly-lit entrance hall, with a flight of stairs disappearing off to the left.

There was nobody in sight. Not even any sound.

Lennie followed his quarry into the building.

He stood absolutely still, listening. Somewhere up above he could hear someone coughing, a half-covered choking sound that was brittle and distant. Aside from that the silence held. Had Charlie stayed on this floor or climbed the stairs?

Lennie heard again the lieutenant's words: don't try to stop him, all I want to know is where he runs to. Lennie already knew that much. If he turned around now and went back to the street, he could use his contact number for the lieutenant and his job would be done. But Lennie couldn't resist trying to discover a little more.

He made up his mind to try the stairs, drawn by a repetition of the harsh coughing he had heard before. The treads of the stairs were bare of any covering save for mud and dust and the dried and darkening splashes of vomit. Here and there dark spots that might have been blood.

Lennie paused at the first landing and listened again. The coughing had subsided and no other sound had risen in its place. He continued to climb.

An empty corridor stretched away to the right; a succession of closed doors, each with a number in fading paint. The panels of at least two of the doors had been kicked through. Lennie moved with caution towards the first of these and bent low enough to look in.

The room was bare; wallpaper peeling away; linoleum had been pulled up from the boards, bits and pieces of it left clinging there. As far as he could see there was no one inside the room. Lennie straightened up and moved on.

A cough and a groan drew him towards the end of the corridor. There was a padlock attached to the door, which was itself intact. Someone had even had a go at repainting it, but got fed up halfway through. The lock itself was unfastened.

Lennie was wondering whether to try the handle or not when he heard the sound of footsteps on the floor below; steps that seemed to be approaching the stairs. His mind had been made up for him. Without any further hesitation, he turned the handle, smiled as it gave against his hand, and stepped swiftly inside the room.

He stood just inside the door, letting his eyes grow accustomed to the light. Razor-thin diagonals of brightness came between the boards which had been nailed to the windows, and in these Lennie picked out several stained mattresses, a tumble of cardboard boxes, squashed and dented cans, the crumpled containers of a couple of dozen takeaway meals. Across the room, an internal door was two-thirds open and from inside there came another wracked cough.

Lennie was listening for any more footsteps outside, but there was nothing.

Another cough, more brutal than before, and his curiosity got the better of him. It was only four paces to the other side of the room and one of them placed his foot down on something that crackled and broke beneath it. Lennie stopped and held his breath.

There was no reaction from beyond the door.

He bent low to see what he had trodden on and made out a shattered hypodermic syringe.

Lennie moved on to the door and eased it open a little further. Immediately he was staring down at the desperate face of a young Puerto Rican, lying in the centre of the floor, his eyes wide and his pupils dilated. Another syringe lay close to his arm — an arm which Lennie could see even in the half light was pockmarked with scars.

The boy tried to lift a hand towards Lennie, but as he did so, another volley of violent coughs shook him much as a dog shakes a rat between its teeth.

Lennie didn't move: he had no idea what to do. Neither did he have a chance to make up his mind.

Even as he was staring back at the boy, the door to the apartment opened.

Lennie froze. He listened breathlessly as whoever had entered walked across the room, following the path Lennie himself had taken. He waited until the door was pushed open and heard the words — 'Luis, what . . .?'

That was all.

Lennie had recognized the newcomer as the Vietnamese boy. He reached out and grabbed his arm, swinging him into the room so that he stumbled over the Puerto Rican's legs. A push was all that was needed to send him to the ground and, before he had landed, Lennie had jumped back through the outer room and was slamming the apartment door behind him. Quick fingers clicked the padlock shut. Lennie ran the length of the corridor; took the stairs three or four at a time. The window he had clambered through was the only one not fully boarded over and it made the best exit.

Within minutes he was walking down the street, feeling in his pockets for a couple of quarters and saying the number Jackie Eves had given him over and over inside his head.

There was an important call he had to make.

* * *

The twins had first met Karen when they arrived in New York and began working in their step-mother's restaurant. Karen was a bright, dark-haired girl around their own age, who Alice treated more like an extra daughter than a member of her staff. Karen responded by working hard, keeping time, and confiding in Alice as if she had been her own mother.

Karen's ambition was to be a photographer. She wouldn't rest until her news pictures had been on the front pages of all the newspapers and magazines in the country and until the major galleries had featured exhibitions of her work.

She was young, but she was keen and talented and she was already well on the way. Keeping up with the twins had helped — on several occasions she had been around with her camera in time to snap a crucial moment in their adventures.

Her trip to Maine had come about as a result of Sam and Lennie, as well. They had gone there to work during the summer and, as often happened, trouble followed them closely. This time, espionage and nuclear secrets had kept them busy and had come close to costing their lives. But the twins had got themselves out of it without serious accident or injury and had helped the security services to capture some spies into the bargain.

They had also met a woman botanist who just happened to be in need of a photographic assistant for one of the projects she was working on. Fine, had been Karen's response, flowers will make a change from taking pictures of hoodlums and punks here in the city.

So it had proved: though now Karen was pleased to

119

be back in New York; pleased to see Alice; to see Ruth. She was so pleased to see Sam that she gave him a big hug and an enthusiastic kiss on the cheek before either she thought about what she was doing or Sam could stop her.

Karen was so carried away by her pleasure at seeing Sam again that she failed to notice that Sam was hardly in the mood for such a friendly greeting. Indeed it was so sudden and surprising that it went a long way to jolting him out of the mood he had become locked away in.

Karen stood there beaming and talking nineteen to the dozen, not noticing that Sam was saying very little. Only when she had told him all about her time up in Downeast Maine — the work she had done, the people she had met — did Karen pause, stand back and draw breath. Only then did she notice that poor Sam was looking slightly shell-shocked.

'Sam,' Karen said, with concern, 'is everything okay? With you, I mean.'

Sam looked at her for some moments and then his mouth moved into what was the closest to a smile he had managed for days. 'Karen,' he said, 'let's go down by the river. Let's go for a walk.'

Walk was what they did; down along the cobbled street and through the fish market, continuing until they reached the edge of the Hudson River itself. Only then did walk become talk.

'I had a letter,' Sam began.

'And it wasn't good news?' Karen said, reading the tone of his voice.

'Not exactly,' said Sam. He fished into the rear pocket of his jeans and brought out the folded envelope and handed it to her: now she could read that as well.

Karen read it twice through and handed it back to Sam without making any comment. They walked on towards the pier, ignoring the gulls that flew close about them.

'Have you tried looking for her?' Karen asked, finally.

Sam shook his head.

'Will you?'

'Where would I try? You know as well as I do how many kids come to the city each year, each month. Besides . . .' Sam looked at Karen, but didn't continue.

'Besides,' she tried for him, 'if she wants to find you, she knows where you are — isn't that what you were going to say?'

'Yes, I suppose so. Something like that.'

'It's upset you, hasn't it, Sam?'

'That Marcie's run off again?'

'No, that she hasn't come to you for help.'

Sam stopped as if he'd run smack into an invisible wall. The thought that had been lingering, unrecognized at the back of his mind, leapt to the front where he could no longer ignore it. 'I guess,' he said slowly, not liking to admit it, 'that it has.'

Karen gave him a soft smile. 'But, Sam, you know what she's like, the kind of a tough girl she is. Just think how hard it is for her to ask anyone for help. Anyone.'

'But I thought she trusted me — I hoped she did.'

'And you were the one who helped her before. If she's got herself into trouble again, she may find it more difficult to come to you than anyone else.

121

That doesn't mean she doesn't trust you, Sam. It doesn't mean she doesn't like you. It's because she *does* that she'd find it so hard to stand face to face with you and ask for help. She'll feel that she's letting you down.'

'That's nonsense!' said Sam, sharply.

'Is it, Sam?'

He walked on for some way after that, thinking about what they both had said, thinking about Marcie, trying to sort out what it was he really felt about her.

'You feel responsible for her, don't you, Sam?'

They were standing at the far end of the pier, looking out over the water to the land at the far side and the Circle Line tour boat that was passing in between.

'Maybe,' he said, grudgingly. 'I suppose . . . yes, in a way . . . though I don't see why . . .'

His sentence faltered into silence.

'It makes perfect sense to me,' said Karen. 'After all, you were the one who saved her life. If it hadn't been for you she would have thrown herself off that bridge and that would have been the end of it. You were the reason she didn't do that, Sam. You *are* responsible for her, like it or not.' For no more than a couple of seconds, Karen squeezed his hand. 'That's a lot for anyone to take on their shoulders, Sam; especially where someone like Marcie is concerned.'

She stood back and waited for him to say something, make some kind of move. When he did it was to tell her that he wanted to be on his own for a time.

'You're sure?'

'I just want to take a walk. I'll see you back at the restaurant.'

122

Karen took a couple of paces back, but then hesitated, uncertain.

'Hey, Karen, I'll be fine. Tell Lennie to hang around so that we can eat together. We've got stuff we ought to talk about. Okay?'

'Okay,' Karen smiled, and walked off the pier in one direction, allowing Sam to walk off in the other.

15

Marcie had spent hour after hour trudging around every bar and club in the city. Guitar slung over her shoulder, she had walked in, asked to see the owner, smiled, talked about how she'd worked in some of the toughest places in the state of Montana and then pulled the quitar round and began to sing.

At least, that was the idea. The reality was somewhat different.

In a lot of places she barely got a foot inside the door. Others didn't seem to have either an owner or a manager around and nobody knew when he or she was coming back. If there was someone for Marcie to talk to, they failed to take her seriously. Some listened for a spell, but then their eyes glazed over, their heads turned and Marcie knew they'd stopped hearing what she was saying. Some just took one look at her scruffy clothes and unkempt hair and laughed full into her face.

Those with patience or a streak of kindness let her get as far as the first bars of a song, before patting her on the shoulder and saying, 'Sorry, kid. No offence, but that's not what we're looking for.'

What were they looking for, Marcie asked them. Whatever it was she was sure she could do it. She had a voice, she could play, why wouldn't somebody give her a chance?

Part of the answer was that there were a whole bunch of singers like Marcie who were out to make a name for themselves in New York — which meant that New York could be choosy. And right then it wasn't prepared to choose Marcie.

The last straw came when she was tossed out of a filthy diner down near the entrance to the Holland Tunnel. Most of the customers were drunken down-and-outs anyway, none of them could have heard the difference between a good note and a hole in the ground. Still, the greasy guy behind the counter had wiped his fat hands down through the stains on his once-white apron and told her to get back out on the streets where she belonged.

So Marcie did exactly that. She found herself a good spot, dropped her leather jacket down inside out to catch the coins, tuned her guitar and started singing.

At first, people walked past with their noses in the air and their feet moving so fast you'd think they were in training for the walkathon. But little by little she began to get some attention; first a dime dropped down into the lining of her coat, then a couple of quarters, finally a dollar. After that there was a slow but fairly steady stream of small change so that by the time Marcie's throat was beginning to feel sore and the tips of her fingers hurt from pushing down on the strings, she had a grand total of twenty-four dollars and seventy-two cents.

With a smile, she walked down the street, went into the first café she came to and ordered a coffee and two (count 'em!) honey-dipped doughnuts.

Bliss!

Marcie sat there, enjoying the fact that she had earned the money herself, savouring the way the honey glaze broke against her mouth, yielding to the soft doughy texture underneath. She loved doughnuts!

She realized, without thinking about doing so, that she was thinking about Sam. Sam Tempest.

She pictured him outside the restaurant where he and his brother worked. Looking directly at her with blue-grey eyes, holding her gaze and not looking away like most people did. He had asked her to trust him. Well, maybe she should have. Trusted him more, that is. Maybe she still could. After all, a girl needed a friend in the big city, didn't she?

Marcie was smiling to herself. She was imagining sitting there in the café with Sam, sharing the doughnuts, the coffee, the conversation.

'Twenty-four bucks, Sam,' she'd say with a proud grin. 'Close to twenty-five. Not bad for a first try, huh?'

And Sam would grin back at her over his coffee cup and say, 'Better than not bad, Marcie. Pretty good.'

That's how it would go, she figured. Something like that. When she saw him again. If . . .

Marcie sprang to her feet. What was she talking about — if? Why shouldn't she go see him now? Right now? While she was in this great mood, while she was feeling on top of things. Yes, why not?

Marcie swallowed down the last of her coffee, called a cheery goodbye to the woman behind the counter, grabbed the last chunk of uneaten doughnut and took it with her out on to the street. Pretty soon she was down at the subway buying a handful of tokens, taking the train out towards Brooklyn Bridge. She could remember exactly where the restaurant was situated, snug there under the shadow of the bridge. All she had to do was walk right in, pushing the doors back with her hands, head up and smiling and come right out with it: 'Hey! Sam around? Tell him an old friend's here to see him from Montana. Marcie's the name. Yes, that's right — Marcie.'

She couldn't do it.

She stood right across the street and watched customers going in through the door; walking back out. She heard the rise and fall of voices, the faint clatter of cutlery against china; she could smell the inviting variety of food smells.

She couldn't bring herself to walk through the door. All of the confidence that she had felt less than half an hour before had evaporated.

Sam wouldn't as much as remember her, she knew it for a fact.

'Marcie?' she could picture him saying. 'Marcie who?'

And if he did remember her, seeing her, there was no way he was going to be pleased that she was there.

'Oh, God!' she could see him saying. 'What's *she* doing here? All that girl means is trouble. Look at what happened last time I got mixed up with her.' And, in Marcie's imagination, he turned fast on his heel and stalked away, leaving her standing there with everyone in the restaurant staring right at her.

Marcie closed her eyes in embarrassment and pain; when she opened them again, she was the one to walk away. She walked down towards the river, through the docks and past the small expensive shops on the boundary of Seaport. Without knowing where she was going, Marcie was heading for the pier. Twenty or so metres along it, she stopped short.

Her mouth was open wide but she was finding it difficult to breath. There, standing at the end of the pier, gazing out over the water, was Sam. And he wasn't alone.

There was a girl with him; a girl around Marcie's own age, but half a head taller, better dressed — not ultra smart, but what she was wearing was clean and looked as if it knew what an iron was all about. Her dark hair lifted a little in the wind and fell back down perfect as she half-turned her head towards Sam and smiled.

Marcie hated the way she smiled! She was sick to her stomach.

The only good thing about it was that, at least, Sam didn't turn his head too and smile back. Instead he kept gazing out over the water like he was thinking important thoughts and the stupid girl carried on grinning at him like she was some kind of two-legged Cheshire cat.

It was all that Marcie could do not to rush up there and push her headlong into the Hudson River.

Then Sam did turn towards her and surely — yes — that was the beginning of a little smile around the edges of his mouth. And now they were talking, nice and easy, talking as if they were used to it, being together that way, talking together. Real nice and easy. Real close.

Marcie's head was swimming.

Of all the fools in the world, she was the biggest — thinking that someone like Sam Tempest would

128

ever think of her; that he would ever remember her, care about her, want to see her again as long as she lived.

Marcie turned away and, half-walking, half-running, made her way through the crowds towards the nearest subway. As she ran she collided first with one person, then another: difficult to see exactly where she was going, half-blinded as she was by tears.

16

'The thing is,' Jackie Eves was saying, 'everything seems to be getting close to boiling point. And quicker than I imagined. Which means we could be in for some pretty big trouble.' She was sitting in the kitchen of the restaurant, having slipped in through the back door under cover of darkness.

Alice had pulled out a table, made up a tomato and garlic sauce for some choice pasta and set it down in front of them for supper.

Sam and Lennie were there, Karen also. Alice drifted in and out, half wanting to know what was going on, while the rest of her thought the least she knew the more comfortable she would feel.

'One of the toughest of the crack gangs,' the lieutenant went on, 'was attacked in the early hours. This club down on the lower east side, there must have been eighty, ninety people in there, all friends. Couple of bodyguards out on the street, another in the hallway.'

She paused, looking at the faces watching her, listening.

'They came in three cars and this time it wasn't just baseball bats and axe handles, though they had those as well. This time the first ones out on the pavement came with sawn-off shotguns poking through the folds of their overcoats. One of the bodyguards was too brave for his own good. Right now surgeons are still picking the pieces of shot out of him in the operating theatre. The others had more sense and stood aside to let the raiders through.

'They were as brutal as they were efficient. It's surprising what you can break apart with a few heavy blows of a blunt instrument: bottles, furniture, heads, fingers.'

Despite herself, Karen shuddered.

'You still think this is Michael Angelo's doing?' asked Sam.

Jackie Eves nodded. 'I don't see who else has the muscle to work this way. The smaller gangs have been warring with each other all the time, but they don't work in this way. Like I say, they don't have the muscle.'

'But you still can't prove it?' Lennie asked.

Jackie Eves smiled, ruefully. 'If I could, I doubt we'd all be sitting here.'

'Why are we?' asked Sam.

'Because I still need something that will link Angelo to some of what's going on. It may not be enough to get him up in front of a judge, but if I can get some leverage from it, maybe I can force him into dropping all this violence. Show him I know a little and let on I can prove more.'

'You mean bluff him,' said Lennie.

'Sure,' said the lieutenant. 'I always was a pretty good poker player. It's one of the few ways a woman officer can get accepted by the men in the station — sitting up with them through the night while the whisky bottle goes down and the stakes go up.' She grinned. 'If I can play poker with some of those tough cops, I'd fancy myself taking Angelo a few hands. But before I can do that I need something to play with. I need some cards.'

'Where are you going to get them from, Lieutenant?' asked Karen.

'Maybe the twins here,' said Jackie Eves. 'Just maybe.'

'Tell me,' said Karen, sitting forward.

'Well, first off, Lennie did a little tracking for me. He let things go to his head, of course, and forgot exactly what his orders were . . .'

Lennie blushed and looked at the floor close to his feet.

'. . . but he found out where one of the kids that the gangs have been using to move their dope around the city lives. Right now I've got the place under surveillance and when the kid pokes his head out again, he'll be followed. He just might lead us somewhere we want to go.

'The other is a long shot, but it may prove to be my ace in the hole. And that's a guy called Fat Freddy. Sam and Lennie were tailing him when he got himself badly beaten up. We think that Freddy might have been working for Angelo. There's a twenty-four hour watch at his bedside, waiting for him to come round long enough to tell us so.'

'You think he will?' asked Sam.

'He just might. Angelo got him out of jail fast enough because he needed him out on the street, but since he landed in hospital, he hasn't been near him. Not as much as a bunch of grapes. He's making it pretty clear that he doesn't want to know.

'As for me, I'm waiting and hoping.'

Lennie forked the last portion of pasta into his

mouth and before he had finished chewing it, asked;
'That can't be all you're going to do.'

'A lot of police work is exactly that. Especially when you're undercover.'

'What if,' said Sam, suddenly, 'while you and your officers are doing the waiting and hoping, Lennie and I think of a little something that might hurry things along?'

The lieutenant sipped at her espresso. The first time she'd tasted Alice's strong black coffee she'd figured it was the best in the city and since then, nothing had happened to change her mind. She hadn't changed her mind about Sam and Lennie either; the Tempest Twins had proved their worth in the past and there was no reason to believe this time would be different. After all, she'd asked them to get involved precisely because, as young people, they could do things and go places that were closed to her officers.

She set her small cup carefully down in its saucer. 'Okay,' she said, slowly, 'why don't you tell me exactly what's on your mind?'

Marcie didn't go straight back to the old apartment building. Instead, she got off the train after a couple of stops and walked and walked until her feet ached more than her head. Only then did she begin to stop thinking about Sam. Sam and the girl, whoever she might have been.

Anger was still high within her, nonetheless, and when she went into the alleyway at the back of the boarded-up building she was far too tense to notice the man sitting in a faded blue Chevvy parked across the street. She didn't notice the small Polaroid camera

133

he lifted to his face, nor the quick movement of his hand as he made notes in the pad down by his side.

Marcie moved across the empty hallway, sneakers sending up clouds of dust as she scuffed them across the floor.

Neb had heard her coming and hurried down the stairs to meet her. 'Hey, Marcie!' he called. 'Where you. . . ?'

Marcie threw out her right arm and punched Neb hard high in the chest. The skinny kid's mouth flew open as he was driven backwards; his legs went from underneath him and he sat down on the edge of the stairs hard.

Marcie turned on the landing and almost ran smack into Charlie, who had hurried out to see what all the commotion was about.

'Hey, girl!' he shouted. 'What's going on?'

'Shut it!' Marcie snapped, swerving round the Vietnamese boy.

But Charlie hadn't had such a good day either. He lunged after Marcie, seizing her arm and spinning her round. His other hand emerged from his side pocket and there was a quick flash as a switchblade darted into sight.

It was all a mistake.

Marcie ducked low, swinging her guitar round from her back and grasping its neck so that she could direct it against Charlie's arm. The side of the guitar body cracked against the boy's elbow and he winced with pain; his fingers flew open and the knife dropped towards the floor. Before it touched, Marcie had drawn back her right foot and kicked forward hard. Her instep landed full-force between the boy's legs.

Charlie screamed and then he did something he

had never done before in his life.

He fainted.

Marcie sneered, swung her guitar back into place and stalked off to the room she had appropriated as her own. 'What a dump!' she called out to the walls as she entered.

She looked around at the sagging couch, the refrigerator that refused to work, the blankets rolled against the wall, the mouse droppings scattered all over. 'What a dump!'

Marcie slammed the door behind her so hard that it came off its upper hinge.

What on earth was she doing here? Sharing this Godforsaken place with a Puerto Rican junkie, a scrawny sneak thief and a refugee from Vietnam who was training hard to be a drug dealer if he ever grew up?

She lay down on the couch and pulled the blankets up over her head.

'Jackie!'

The lieutenant paused at the back door and waited for Sam to catch up with her.

'Can we talk?'

She looked at him curiously. 'I thought that's what we'd been doing.'

'Sure. Only I mean . . .'

'About something else?'

'Someone else.'

Jackie Eves raised an eyebrow. 'Anything to do with the case?'

Sam shook his head. 'I hope not.'

'In that case, anyone I know?'

Sam nodded.

'Out with it then. Not like you to be shy with words.'

Sam looked into the lieutenant's face. 'You remember Marcie?'

'The girl you talked down off the bridge?'

Sam nodded again.

'Sure I remember her. Went back out west. What about her?'

'She came back east.'

'Here to New York?'

'I think so. Least her folks think so. They wrote to me.'

Jackie Eves looked sympathetic. 'What do you want me to do, Sam?'

'I thought maybe you could get her photograph printed up from the files, run it past missing persons and maybe let your own undercover team have copies too.'

The lieutenant touched Sam lightly on the arm. 'Sure. Why not? Can't do any harm.' She took a step away. 'And Sam . . . you and Lennie, take care, won't you? There've been enough casualties in this affair as it is.'

'Don't worry,' Sam replied. 'We don't take any risks we don't have to.'

Jackie Eves grinned, raised a hand in salute and melted into the darkness.

'Marcie! Marcie!'

Neb knocked on the door, careful not to bang too hard for fear that it would fall off the other hinges and cease to function altogether. 'Hey, Marcie! Listen up.'

There was no way of knowing if she was listening or not. Neb put his face close against the gap between door edge and frame. He could just make out Marcie's shape, sitting on the couch with what looked like blankets draped right over her head.

'Marcie!' He hissed. 'This is important!'

Still the shape refused to move.

'Marcie, you want to make fifty bucks?'

Nothing.

'Fifty dollars, Marcie, just for a half hour's work. Less than that. Marcie? All you got to do is make a delivery. It's for Charlie. Charlie can't go. You could. Uptown a few blocks. You can take a cab if you want. Take a cab and take this package. Fifty dollars. Come on, Marcie. That's more than you can make standing out with your guitar in a whole day. Two days.'

The shape beneath the blankets had not budged and, for one moment, Neb thought she might have died. But then he figured that anyone who was dead wouldn't be able to keep themselves so upright from the waist.

'Marcie!' he tried once more. 'Ain't you going to do it? Fifty dollars!'

Still nothing.

Neb scratched his head, failing to understand, and turned back into the hall. Women, he was thinking. Girls! How were you ever supposed to know what was going on in their minds?

17

Neb had to leave the house some time. The twins had figured that after the previous day's lucky escape the Vietnamese boy was unlikely to be taking risks. Of course, there were probably others living there, but from what they'd seen of Neb, he wasn't the kind to stay cooped up for too long.

It was one of those grey days in the city when a mist of cloud hung over the tops of the buildings like opaque sheeting. Damp was beginning to eat into their bones as they hunched in the doorway along the street and waited.

From that position they could see the end of the alley which led to the back of the building, as well as the unmarked car in which the undercover police were carrying out their photographic surveillance.

'You know what we should have done?' asked Sam, rubbing his hands against his legs to keep the circulation flowing.

'Brought a Thermos of hot coffee?'

'Yes, but that wasn't what I meant.'

'Worn an extra sweater?'

'Right again, but still not what I was thinking of.'

'So tell me.'

'We should have checked with the lieutenant and

gone through the pictures they're taking. We just might have recognized some of Neb's callers.'

'Good thinking,' agreed Lennie. 'Why doesn't one of us do that now? There doesn't seem a lot of point in us both hanging on here.'

'You mean,' said Sam, knowing his brother only too well, 'why don't *you* go.'

'Sure. Why not? I can bring us back a couple of coffees, what's wrong with that?'

'Nothing,' said Sam, with a grin.

'So what's that sarcastic look for?'

'It's funny the way you find it impossible to stay still and patient for more than half an hour at a time.'

'I'm still when I sleep,' said Lennie.

'Sometimes.'

'And what's that supposed to mean?'

'Last night you were turning and calling out and kicking off the covers like you were in the middle of World War Three.'

'No,' Lennie smiled. 'I was playing quarterback for the Washington Redskins. We were at the superbowl and there were three mintues left in the last quarter . . .'

'Enough,' hissed Sam suddenly. 'We don't even have three minutes. Look.'

Lennie turned his head in time to see the thin shape of Neb darting out from the alley and immediately heading along the street towards them.

'Back!' said Lennie, urgently.

The twins flattened themselves against the inside wall and held their breaths as Neb went past on the opposite pavement. He was walking quickly, breaking into a little run every ten metres or so, then stopping himself and dropping back to a walk.

'Doesn't want to draw attention to himself,' whispered Sam.

'Too late for that,' said Lennie.

'Wait till he gets to the end of the block,' said Sam, 'then you take one side of the street, I'll take the other. Remember, he's seen me before. The last thing we want is to mess this up by being recognized.'

'Know something?' said Lennie, looking across at him.

'No. What?'

'You talk too much. Let's go.'

They moved stealthily out from the doorway and set off to tail Neb to wherever he might lead them.

Neb had too many things on his mind. One was Fat Freddy. He'd met Freddy one lazy afternoon in Washington Square. Neb had picked the wrong guy's pocket and, if Freddy hadn't intervened, Neb would have had his head broken open against a paving stone, there and then. It was Freddy who had given him a little streetwise coaching in who it was safe to rob and who it wasn't; which stores had private surveillance people working them and which didn't; what was an easy take. Most times Freddy was right. In the case of Alice's Restaurant he'd been wrong, but that was bad luck waking up those stupid Brits, nothing else.

It was Freddy who'd started to cut Neb in on pushing the dope. Well, not pushing it exactly. More making a delivery. There were already lots of people out on the street waiting to score; lots of middle-men eager to buy the stuff and steel it again. Like the pretzel guy from Battery Park, the one Charlie had been making a delivery to when suddenly the whole place had been swarming with cops. Charlie maybe didn't have such good luck either. Fancy making it out of Saigon on some leaky tub just when the whole place was about to go up in flames, staying alive somehow while they drifted over the ocean for weeks without any decent supplies, catching hold of a piece of wood when the boat finally sank and then drifting and clinging on to that for almost a week till a fishing boat hauled you on board like you were bait and took you into Hong Kong harbour. Fancy doing all that, Neb thought, and then ending up getting shot by a juggler who turns out to be a policeman in disguise.

Not that Charlie had been shot. Not that time.

But it was getting more and more difficult; more and more dangerous. People stabbing one another in the back, cutting one another's throats. And now that mobster that Freddy had got involved with was trying to take over the whole thing.

Another mistake, Neb figured, to get mixed up with someone from the Mafia. And he had always thought that Freddy knew what he was doing — perhaps he did until those guys jumped him up in Harlem and pounded him within an inch of his life with tyre irons.

Now Freddy was in bed in the hospital, tubes coming and going from just about every part of his body and a twenty-four hour police guard waiting for his last word, even if that was only goodbye.

It was a hell of a life, thought Neb. One hell of a way to die.

He checked, realized that he'd walked one block too many, turned and doubled back — was that someone along the street, someone watching him? — aiming for the place where he hoped he would find the girl.

Neb walked with special care, checking behind in the reflections of store windows, looking back over his shoulder whenever he changed direction. No, there wasn't anybody. Just a bunch of people out in the city doing whatever people did. He wasn't being followed, he was pretty sure of that.

He made two more turns and ran down the iron steps which led to the basement kitchen of a small pizza place. He rubbed some of the mist and dirt away from the outside of the window and peered through. At first he thought she wasn't there, but then he spotted her, a tiny figure behind the huge sink, smaller and skinnier than himself even. Her sleeves were pushed high on her arms and her hands were submerged in soapy water as they washed their way through pile after pile of plates.

Neb tapped on the window, but she didn't hear him. Someone else in the kitchen was singing along to the radio and that, added to the clatter of plates, made if difficult.

He tapped again, louder this time, and a bearded man wearing a dirty white overall, a matching chef's hat, and with a cigarette hanging from one corner of his mouth, came towards the window. 'Whatchawant?'

The cigarette wobbled and an inch and a half of pale grey ash fell away.

Neb pointed towards the sink.

'Youwannajob? No job.'

Neb shook his head and pointed again.

'Youwannagirl?'

Neb nodded.

The man shrugged his heavy shoulders, wandered to the sink and tapped the girl on the arm, then jerked his head in the direction of the window.

She saw who it was and a plate slithered soapily through her fingers and broke into pieces against the tiled floor.

Sam moved so slowly it was if he wasn't moving at all. One eye peeked around the edge of the wall and down the curve of iron steps that led to the basement. There was Neb, bending forward, talking urgently to someone who had obviously come from inside the building. He could see from the position of Neb's body, the way he kept gesticulating first with one hand and then the other, that he was putting everything into getting something his own way.

Sam held his breath and pulled his head away.

Lennie made a face that meant, what's happening?

Sam used his fingers to show that Neb was talking and then shrugged and raised his eyebrows to show that he didn't yet know what they were talking about. He looked again and, by now, the couple had altered their positions; not much, just enough to allow Sam to see who Neb was speaking to.

Sam's eyes widened.

It was Zoe. The girl from the zoo. The frightened little kid who just wanted to be child again; the one who wanted to talk to the animals.

Her dark eyes were wide and she was shaking her head so vigorously from side to side, Sam thought she must be in danger of giving herself a headache.

Neb got hold of her thin arms and pressed his

fingers against them hard enough to make the girl wince. There were not many people around, Sam thought, who were small enough for Neb to bully.

After several minutes — interrupted by a couple of increasingly impatient shouts from the kitchen — Zoe seemed to agree. Neb took a taped package, not much larger than a paperback book from inside his zip-up jacket and handed it to Zoe, who immediately shoved it inside her top.

As Sam watched, Neb reached back inside his jacket and took out a fifty-dollar bill which he held for several seconds in front of Zoe's face.

When she reached out for it, he laughed and pulled it away; she snatched at it again, and again Neb was too quick for her. After the girl's third attempt, Neb taunted her with it once more and then tore the bill in half. Zoe gasped and stood there open-mouthed.

Neb gave her one half of the bill and this time he spoke loudly enough for Sam to hear what he said distinctly: 'When you've delivered.'

He was still laughing as he turned away.

Sam was just able to duck back from sight in time, gesturing to Lennie to move fast. They were several buildings along the street before Neb surfaced. But he didn't go far. He wandered off in the other direction and then loitered around, waiting for something to happen.

He didn't have to wait long.

Inside five minutes, Zoe appeared. She came up from the basement at a run, turned towards where the twins were hiding and hurried past them so close that either Sam or Lennie could have reached out a hand and touched her.

They watched her instead; saw Neb, satisfied that his mission was being carried out, head off in the opposite direction. Lennie looked at his brother questioningly.

Sam pointed after Zoe and Lennie nodded, slipping out after her. Sam waited several moments then began following Neb. One of them, at least, had to be leading the twins somewhere interesting.

18

Neb didn't waste a lot of time. Just enough to buy a twenty-five cent bar of chocolate and steal milk, bread, jam and eggs. Once that was done with, he headed back to the apartment fast. In through the rear window and, after that, nothing.

Sam sighed and looked above his head. The clouds had barely shifted in the past hour. The air was still cold and damp although there was nothing as definite as rain.

He looked across at the boarded-up building and decided that he was in for a long wait and he'd have to make the best of it. Why had he been so stupid as to leave his book behind?

Zoe was nervous at the best of times and this certainly wasn't the best of times. Whatever she was carrying, it was hotter than the hottest of hot bricks. Several times she darted out into traffic and on each occasion she was lucky not to get knocked over. One burly cab driver was so incensed that he braked to a squealing halt and left his passengers stranded in the rear while he cursed Zoe and several generations of her ancestors, finding plenty of fault with all of them.

If Zoe was worried about this, she paid no

attention. The man's words skipped off her like stones on moving water. She had more to concern herself with than mere words.

Sticks and stones, Lennie thought, following; sticks and stones.

He waited until she was safely across the street and then hurried after her, having to jump fast to avoid colliding with a roller skater who was gliding between the traffic at some speed. Lennie shouted out an apology and the skater responded with a shrill blast of the whistle that hung by a brightly-coloured cord from round his neck.

Just that swing of the head and Lennie thought that he had lost her; but no, there she was up ahead of him, dodging in and out of the busy shoppers and business girls striding out in their smart suits but with sneakers on their feet. High heels were strictly for the office, not for walking around the city.

Zoe stopped so suddenly that Lennie was caught off guard and had to dive into the front of a hair-dressing salon which seemed to specialize in straightening naturally curly hair. Photographs of beautiful women and handsome men stared out at him from beneath a sign which read 'Straight and Narrow'.

Lennie looked along the street and saw that Zoe was bending down towards a shop window, her forehead resting against the glass. The sign that hung out over the entrance was moving lightly in the wind and, on it, a painted bird sat happily on the head of a large white dog.

Zoe pushed herself away from the window and carried on up the street. When Lennie drew level with the shop he saw that what she had been fascinated by were four brown and white puppies, all of them looking cuddly and curled up inside thick straw.

The impression of Zoe's fingermarks and the last faint clouds of her breath was just visible still on the windowpane.

Zoe's destination was a corner store that sold second-hand records and video tapes, cheap stereos and automatic toasters. The windows were decorated with posters of David Bowie and Madonna, Marilyn Monroe and James Dean. They had been there for so long that they were beginning to fade and to peel back at the edges.

A punk with swastikas dangling from his torn leather jacket and bleached hair, cut to a quarter inch from his scalp, sat on the pavement outside, turning the beads of a rosary over and over between his fingers.

Lennie wondered who he was praying for and wondered if it was himself.

Inside the store there were a few more punks, idly leafing through the rack of albums. A girl who would have been a pretty decent stand-in for Miss Universe stood gazing up at a picture of Janis Joplin, smoking a cigarette and singing *Ball and Chain*. Down at the counter a middle-aged woman with make-up that was inches thick and a threadbare fur coat was demanding a copy of *Al Martino's Greatest Hits*, over and over and over again.

'Lady,' said the man serving. 'He never had that many hits and, if he did, he never deserved 'em.'

The man had a mostly bald head that shone like a well-groomed billiard ball; his white shirt looked like it had come back from the laundry no more than an hour previously and the heavy chain of a gold fob watch hung over the pockets at the front of his blue pinstriped waistcoat.

Lennie moved towards the heavy metal section and began to check out the Motorhead L.P.s, at the same time as watching Zoe, who was clearly deciding whether to approach the man now or to wait until the Al Martino fan had lost interest.

'Come on, lady,' said the man, finally. 'There's other customers here.'

'I'm a customer,' said the woman, firmly.

'Sure, sure. Only some of the others, they're from this century.'

'Wise guy, huh!' she said, and shrugged her coat back on her shoulders.

The girl with the muscles and the cigarette had finished with *Ball and Chain* and was starting on *Piece of My Heart*.

One of the punks had found a Johnny Rotten album and was throwing it across to one of his friends.

'Hey!' shouted the man at the counter. 'Cut that out!'

The punk turned to glare at him and missed the record, which skidded out of its cover and along the floor.

'Okay, okay!' shouted the man. 'You paid for that!'

'Yeah,' said the punk. 'Great!' and he scooped it up from the floor and laughed at his mates as they began to shuffle towards the door.

'Get back here!' yelled the man.

'Gimme *Al Martino's Greatest Hits*!' insisted the woman in the fur coat.

At the top of her voice Miss Junior America was

149

begging all and sundry to take another little piece of her heart.

By the door assorted punks were gobbing and swearing and pogoing up and down on the Johnny Rotten album.

In one corner of the store, Zoe stood and watched and waited.

In the opposite corner, just out of Zoe's eyeline behind the racks, Lennie did the same.

All it needed was for the automatic toasters to start popping up and they would be having a full-scale riot.

Back at the apartment building, Sam was getting colder and more bored by the minute. He guessed that Neb and whoever else was inside were eating the bread and jam and generally having a fine time. Down the street, one undercover officer slid out from the off-side of the parked car and another took his place.

Sam decided he could do worse than ask about the polaroid photos: it didn't look as if a lot else was about to happen.

The newly-arrived officer was in his mid twenties and was already combing his moustache in the rear-view mirror. His ambition in life was clearly to look like Magnum and he wasn't going to rest until he'd succeeded. From what Sam could see, he'd got the moustache about right, but as far as the rest was concerned he'd have to save up for plastic surgery.

'Hi,' said Sam, leaning down towards the window.

The cop said nothing.

'Hi,' said Sam, again.

The cop grunted something inaudible, took out a small pair of scissors and began to trim the ends of his moustache.

'I'm Sam Tempest,' said Sam, encouragingly.

'Drop dead, kid!' the policeman mumbled, concentrating on the far left side of his upper lip.

'Maybe Lieutenant Eves mentioned me,' Sam said.

'If so,' said the cop, 'I forget.'

'I understand; too many other things to keep in mind, more important.'

'That's right, kid.'

'Like clipping your moustache.'

The man shot him a filthy look. 'You trying to be funny?'

Sam shook his head.

'That's good. 'Cause if I thought you were . . .'

'I'm just trying to get a look at the photographs.'

The policeman put his scissors down on the adjacent seat. 'Which photographs?'

'The ones you and your colleagues are taking of the place across the street.'

'And what do you know about that?'

'I told you, the lieutenant . . .'

'And I told you, clear out and let me get on with my work.'

'But . . .'

'But nothing! Now quit! Skedaddle! Scram! Vamoose!'

Sam sighed and walked away. He would have to wait until somebody else came on duty or the lieutenant herself came by. As he was straightening and about to move away from the window his eyes passed over the rear seat where a bundle of Polaroids was poking out from inside a large envelope. And there, not at the top, but a couple down, only a glimpse of her, part of a head, some hair, one of a pair of oddly bright green eyes

. . . Sam's heart seemed to stop: could it really be Marcie?

Back at Bedlam Records the bald owner stood back and shook his head. From the doorway the punks laughed and jeered. Lennie watched as Zoe plucked up enough courage to approach him.

'What do you want, kid?' he asked, sourly. '*Nellie the Elephant*?'

Zoe's lip puckered but she reached inside her top and drew out the sealed package.

The man's eyes grew visibly brighter.

'I see. You ain't buying, you're selling.' He lifted up a flap in the counter. 'Come back here, sister. Let's do this little piece of business away from all these crazies.'

Zoe hesitated, uncertain; she glanced over her shoulder and as she did so Lennie dropped to his hands and knees behind the record stack.

'Come on,' said the man, 'I ain't gonna bite you.'

Zoe bit down into her lower lip and stepped through to the other side of the counter.

Lennie lifted his head a fraction to see what was going on. As he did so there was a shout from the punks in the doorway and one of them went sprawling back into the middle of the store, arms flying. He tried to steady himself against a record stand and only managed to send the whole thing crashing to the floor.

One of the other punks shouted out and raised his fists and, the next thing he knew, he was stumbling backwards with blood streaming from a broken nose.

The Al Martino fan took one look at the blood and almost fainted away.

Miss Junior America stopped singing so abruptly that she bit her tongue.

The owner's face had drained of all its colour. Every drop.

Lennie didn't dare move.

Four men had pushed their way inside the store, each of them wearing black canvas jeans, black T-shirts and black sweatbands on their wrists; they had black and white basketball boots on their feet and most of their heads were covered by black balaclavas.

The two at the front were wielding lethal-looking tyre irons and the couple covering them from the doorway were carrying sawn-off shotguns.

They didn't say a word: they didn't need to.

The lead pair pushed their way to the counter and vaulted over it. The owner tried to make a dash for it but he'd left it till the last moment. A length of iron went crashing down against the back of his unprotected head and felled him like an ox.

A black gloved hand snatched up the packet.

At that moment Zoe made her bid to escape. She dived between the legs of the nearest man and ducked underneath the counter flap. One of the men went after her and jumped back across the counter; he swung his tyre iron and, had it landed, the force of the blow would have lifted Zoe off her feet. But the woman in the fur coat did a sudden and brave thing. She grabbed one of the toasters that was on the counter and threw it right at the man's face. She was only five or six feet away and it would have been difficult to miss.

He was so startled that he opened his fingers and the iron bar went sailing through the air and crashed into the wall on the far side of the store.

Zoe glanced over her shoulder and then sprinted for the door.

The man who'd been hit with the toaster cursed and clawed the Balaclava from his head. The corner of the toaster had struck him alongside the eye and blood was running freely down the side of his face.

Lennie watched with baited breath to see if the guards in the doorway would use their shotguns on the fleeing girl, but they decided that she wasn't worth the trouble. They would grab her instead.

Before they could do that, the bleeding man swung his open hand at the woman in the fur coat and connected with the side of her face. She went cannoning back against the counter, screaming as she went. The man went after her but he'd reckoned against Miss Junior America, who landed one punch low in his stomach and, as he bent forward, rabbit punched him hard on the back of the neck.

Zoe ducked beneath one pair of grasping arms and swerved inside another.

'Get her!' yelled one of them.

'Don't let her get away!' called another.

Zoe eluded them both. She hurtled out through the front of the store and across the pavement; she was so terrified, so eager to get clear that she kept on running. She ran out into the street, not looking in either direction, only wanting to get away from the men with the black clothes and the guns, only wanting to escape from all this trouble and danger. All she wanted to do was get away. All she wanted to be — all that she had ever wanted to be — was safe.

The driver of the truck had been behind the wheel since seven that morning and he was tired, but even if his reflexes had been sharper it was doubtful if he could have changed direction or hit his brakes in time. There were a dozen witnesses and all of them swore that it was never his fault. The girl just came flying out, right in front of him. The guy never stood a chance.

Nor did Zoe.

Lennie heard the sickening impact of the collision and ran for the street.

By the time he got there the driver was staring down through the windscreen of his tall cab and Zoe's crumpled body was little more than a heap of soiled clothing and shattered bones that lay in the middle of the broad road, silently leaking blood.

One arm was fastened tight about her, as if trying vainly to keep herself together; the other was outstretched and, between its fingers, lightly fluttered one torn half of a fifty-dollar bill.

19

Sam couldn't get the image of Marcie out of his mind. It was hard for him to believe that she was in some way involved with whatever was going on inside the old apartment building, and yet there could be no disputing the evidence of that photograph. There could be no mistaking the look on Marcie's face — the vivid green of her eyes.

When Sam had first bumped into her before, she had been running with a gang of kids who specialized in riding the Staten Island Ferry. They would sing and dance, do anything to draw a crowd, at which point some of the gang would mix with their audience and relieve them of their wallets, watches, whatever they could take that was worth taking.

But this — this was altogether more serious. Lennie had tracked the Vietnamese boy to the building and it was clear that he was one of the people in the drug delivery chain.

And then there was Neb. Neb was in there, too, and it was more than likely that his illegal activities amounted to more than walking off with a couple of blueberry pies.

Jackie Eves had told them that their surveillance suggested one of the other kids living there was a known user of hard drugs, a Puerto Rican named Luis.

Now Marcie.

Sam knew that what he should do was use the contact number for the lieutenant and tell her about Marcie's involvement, ask her what to do. But he was afraid she would say he had to wait, that it was a shame about Marcie, but to be honest Marcie didn't matter. There were other, more important things at stake.

Sam couldn't believe that. He could see the logic of it, but inside himself he couldn't believe it. To him, Marcie did matter.

Maybe Karen had been right — when he had saved her life he had become responsible for her.

'We ain't asking you to go out of your way and try and find her, nor nothing like that . . . maybe you'd be as kind as to ask her to drop us a line, let us know she's safe.'

Sam checked his watch. There was no way of telling how long Lennie would be off following Zoe. Ten minutes past the hour: Sam thought that Marcie could be running out of time.

He had to walk four blocks before finding a hardware store and then waste precious minutes haggling with the woman behind the counter in order to buy a ten dollar, ninety-five cents claw hammer for ten dollars, fifty, which was all the cash he had on him.

When he arrived back at the apartment building a light drizzle had started to fall. Sam wandered up and down in front of the building a couple of times, figuring out which of the boarded windows was the easiest to break his way through. He realized that, if he went in through the rear, the undercover cop in the car would see him, probably (if he could drag his mind away from his moustache), report back to the lieutenant, and that might bring Jackie Eves down there too soon.

Sam needed to make time for himself if he was to succeed.

He decided that the far-corner window was his best bet. Aside from the usual spray-paint writing, somebody had made a half-hearted attempt to set fire to the boards there. One third of the boards were blackened and charred, which should mean they would be easier to shift.

What he didn't want to happen was rouse some over-zealous member of the neighbourhood watch scheme and end up getting put inside for breaking and entering. But then he told himself most people probably didn't give two cents what happened to that building. After all, it was due to be demolished and anything that helped that operation on its way, well, what did that matter?

Sam strolled towards the window as nonchalantly as he could, vaulted over the debris at the edge of the pavement, inserted the claws of the hammer behind the corner of burnt board and pulled back with all his strength.

At first nothing seemed to budge and he was worried that he had underestimated the ease of his task.

He placed the sole of one foot flat against the wall and heaved again. This time there was a satisfying creak and he felt a definite movement beneath the head of the hammer.

Cheered on by this, he pried at the same corner until it was angled several inches out from the wall. Immediately, he attacked the board below it and then the board below that. Seconds folded into minutes, sweat gathered beaneath Sam's arms and at the small of his back. It ran across his forehead and stung his eyes till he wiped it clear with his sleeve.

A portly man wearing a checked cap paused in the middle of walking his portly dog and glanced over at what Sam was doing. Sam carried on working, waiting for the man to call out, to question him. But as soon as the dog had finished doing what dogs do, the man carried on his way without uttering a word.

Sam gave an extra pull and the centre board came clear away at one end. All he needed was to shift the other boards back far enough to allow him entry and that would be that.

Sweat was trickling down his back now.

He couldn't believe that half the street wasn't lined up watching him; at least, that they didn't have their faces pressed against their windows, hands reaching out for their telephones. 'Hello, operator? Give me Emergency. Yes, Police. There's one of those young hoodlums breaking into the building across the way. Yes, that's right. In broad daylight. I don't know what this city is coming to!'

But Sam didn't glance over his shoulder and no police sirens could be heard approaching from the distance. He pushed two lengths of board back with his right arm and clambered up level with the window. One moment and he had jumped through.

Darkness.

Silence.

Only the light fall of his own feet as they landed

159

on the floor — that and the creak of the boards as they swung partly shut behind him.

As he waited for his eyes to grow accustomed to the light, Sam slid the hammer down inside his belt, so that it swung from the head.

Marcie had not slept all night. Every time her eyes had closed, images appeared on the inside of their lids: her mother, weary at the table preparing the supper; her father at the door to the hen house, shading his face from the sun; snow; the view from the bridge she had been clinging to, ready to hurl herself down on to the road and the traffic beneath; Sam's hand as he stretched it out towards her; snow.

Marcie could not understand why she had been dreaming of snow. Why it had frightened her so.

Snow that stretched out across the plains as far as the eye could see. Snow like a carpet, a blanket, an ocean. Snow of the crisp white sheet as it was drawn slowly over the body and face of someone who lay dead.

Marcie jumped as a hand touched her. Shouted.

'Hey! It's okay.' She saw that the Puerto Rican boy had come silently into her room; that now he was crouching on the floor beside her couch. 'It's cool.'

He opened his mouth in a smile and showed where his two front teeth were missing, knocked out in a fight.

Marcie stared at him, surprised that he was still alive. When she had seen him last, stretched out in his own vomit, hung out, withdrawn, she would have sworn he was as close to death as a living person could be.

But now his eyes shone with a more than natural

brightness and, as he gazed at her, the point of his tongue flicked out between his lips, darted through the gap in his teeth like a lizard flickering out between dry stone rocks.

'Hey, Marcie! You feeling pretty bad, huh?'

Marcie tried to turn over on to her side and her stomach made a protesting sound. She realized that Luis was right, she was feeling pretty bad. Her limbs were sore, she was cramping up. The lack of sleep weighed heavy on her and she had to concentrate even to stay awake.

'You know, I got just the thing. For you, you know. Make you feel better.' Luis reached into the breast pocket of his soiled shirt. 'Make you feel good.'

He had a small foil-wrapped packet between his fingers. He smiled at her as he carefully set the foil on the floor and unfolded it. 'See!'

Marcie looked down at the white powder that lay inside the foil. She watched as Luis bent forward over it, watched as his tongue snaked out, flicking a few grains back into his mouth.

'For you, baby. I bring for you.'

Marcie looked at the powder, looked at Luis, slowly shaking her head.

'Come on.'

'No.'

'Come on.'

'No.'

'Come on!'

The word froze on Marcie's lips. No: snow.

For a moment she was back in her dream, rocked in pain, tired, aching, unable to sleep.

Luis was stroking her arm and she looked down

at his fingers but it was as though it was somebody else's arm being stroked, not her own.

'Try it. You see. All this pain. Just a little of this will take it all away. Try.'

Marcie looked at Luis, looked at the powder. Had she ever seen anything so inviting, so white? He was still stroking her arm and it felt good. His fingers were cool. Perhaps the powder was cool too. Cool like snow. Perhaps he was right, it would make her feel good; it would ease away the pain and then she could sleep. More than anything in the world she wanted to sleep.

'Come,' breathed Luis, his voice soft, caressing. 'Come.'

Marcie reached out her hand.

'No!'

She looked up, startled. A different voice, not soft but strong and urgent.

'No, Marcie. Don't do it.'

She wiped at her eyes; it looked like Sam, but she knew it couldn't be. What would Sam be doing there? He didn't know where she was; didn't know and didn't care.

'Don't do it, Marcie.'

Had he spoken again, or was it an echo inside her head? *'Don't do that!'*

She felt she was no longer lying there on the couch inside that stinking building; she was up there on the bridge, clinging to an iron railing, the wind cold and tugging at her, trying to prise her free.

'What difference does it make to you if I live or die?'

'A lot. More than I could say right now.'

Marcie's hand was still reaching out, but now it was towards him. 'Sam,' she said.

Luis sprang to his feet and jumped between them. Almost without thought, Sam swiped him aside with a sweep of his left hand. 'Come on, Marcie. Let's get out of here!'

He caught hold of her arm and pulled her to her feet; she was so light it was like lifting air. The white powder scattered beneath their feet.

'I don't think so,' said Charlie's voice from the doorway. He had a knife in his hand and a look in his eye that said he meant trouble.

Sam had had enough trouble for one day. He pulled the claw hammer from his belt and showed it to the Vietnamese. 'If you don't chuck that knife down the hall and get out of our way, I'm going to use this on your head,' he said.

It took Charlie around five seconds to believe him.

The knife clattered along the filthy hallway and Charlie stepped aside. Sam took Marcie past him and looked at her questioningly.

She pointed right and they moved quickly, down the stairs and into the back room where a skinny kid was doing his best to hide behind a pile of boxes rotting with garbage.

'Out of there, Neb,' said Sam, smartly. 'You're coming with us. Now!'

He kicked away the top boxes and yanked Neb out by his collar. 'There's somebody who wants to hear what you've got to say. All of it.'

'This way,' said Marcie, from over by the rear window. 'We can get through here.'

Sam nodded. 'Fine. Why don't you go first. We'll follow.'

The undercover cop in the parked car had got bored

with trimming his moustache and now he was paring his finger nails. An officer who looks neat and tidy at all times is sure of a promotion, he remembered somebody saying. He just couldn't recall who. But he soon dropped the nail scissors when he saw first one, then two, then three people making an exit from the building. His Polaroid camera was quickly working overtime. One, two, three, got 'em!

He set the camera aside to watch where they were going and a slow look of surprise slid over his face as he realized they were heading straight for him.

20

The first police car to pull up at the accident contained two familiar faces. Armstrong Cutler switched off the siren as he pushed open the door. One glance took in the body, the other spotted Lennie standing close by, looking down at the dead Zoe. Jed Chambers, only moments behind him, also saw the girl lying there in the street, and figured that the large man leaning back against the truck was the driver who had been involved.

'Okay, folks,' called Cutler. 'Let's have some room here. Push back and give us some space.'

He knew that within minutes other cars would arrive and other officers would make the crowd stand respectfully at the far side of a hastily erected cordon.

'Shall I take the driver?' Jed Chambers asked.

Armstrong Cutler nodded. 'Be my guest.'

He knew that the young rookie didn't want to do the other job — didn't want to check the body.

Cutler knelt alongside Zoe and tried not to think about how young she looked. He felt almost tenderly at the pulse that no longer beat at her neck; he remained kneeling longer than was strictly necessary, in the attitude of a man in prayer.

When at last he looked up it was towards Lennie. 'Ambulance?'

Lennie nodded and at that moment the sound of its siren was heard approaching.

'You see what happened?'

'Yes. I mean, not exactly. I . . . but, yes; I know what happened, pretty much. I know why . . . why she was running. Who she was running away from.'

Armstrong Cutler waited. He could see that Lennie was upset, that it was only a matter of time before the tears he'd so far refused to cry would fall.

'I think,' Lennie said, 'I think maybe if you could call the lieutenant . . .'

'Lieutenant Eves?'

Lennie nodded.

'What's she got to do with this?'

'Call her,' said Lennie, sharply. And then, realizing he had raised his voice, he added, 'Please.'

Cutler looked at Lennie's face: the kid wasn't fooling. He turned and walked smartly back to his car radio.

'I'm sorry about the little girl — what's her name? — Zoe — I'm sorry about her.'

Jackie Eves was sitting in the back of the car. She was wearing a jacket in black leather over a thick red shirt; her jeans were faded and tucked into knee-length leather boots. Her hair was pinned close to her head and she looked as if she meant business.

'I keep thinking . . .' Lennie began.

'Don't,' the lieutenant said.

'If I'd done something instead of just standing there.'

'If you'd done anything, anything at all, one of those hoods would have emptied his shotgun at you and then there'd have been all hell to pay. As it is . . .' She paused and let the sentence trail away.

'As it is,' Lennie finished for her, 'Zoe's in the morgue.'

'And you're alive,' said Sam.

Lennie turned on him, angrily. 'What's that supposed to mean? You're allowed to go round on some white charger saving girls left, right and centre, and I'm not. What are you anyway? Some kind of damned Sir Lancelot?'

'Enough!' said Jackie Eves, leaning forward to separate the twins who were in the front and back seats respectively.

Sam and Lennie glared at one another for a few moments and then sat back.

'We've got trouble enough of our own. Either of you two, you want to take a swing at somebody, you'll get your chance any time now. Okay?'

'Okay,' the twins mumbled together.

'All right. Lennie, what you have to remember, it's on account of you that we can make our move. For the first time we have somebody who can make a positive identification on one of these murdering thugs. You wouldn't be a lot of good to us if you were a dead witness now, would you?'

Lennie grunted.

'Added to which, there's more good news for a change. It looks as though your pal Fat Freddy's going to pull through. He came out of his coma today for long enough to whisper a few things about his pal, Michael Angelo. Like the name of the place he meets with his friends, for instance. The friends who go round in Balaclava helmets waving tyre irons.'

Sam leaned forward again. 'Surely it wasn't Angelo's people who jumped Freddy? I thought he was working for him.'

'So he was, but seems Freddy was getting a little greedy. Trying to play both ends off against the middle. He'd finger one of the crack gangs to Angelo, and then he'd get money from the gang for letting them know they were going to be hit. Michael Angelo found out.'

'And he didn't like it,' said Sam.

'He did not. But now with Freddy prepared to make a sworn statement and Lennie our prime witness, we've got something to move on.'

Sam and Lennie were smiling again.

'Okay,' said Jackie Eves. 'This is the way we'll do it.'

Karen pushed open the door to her tiny rented flat and stood to one side, waiting for Marcie to step through. By the time both girls were in the main room it looked overcrowded. Already there were a small stove, a fridge, a cupboard for storing tinned food and plates and mugs; there were a small folding table, a couple of folding chairs and a few stacks of paperback books. Karen's photographs, blown up, decorated the walls. The second room was a bathroom which doubled as Karen's darkroom.

'Where's the bed?' asked Marcie, once she had got her bearings.

Karen pointed to the narrow space between the fridge and the cupboard. 'One folding bed, pulls out from there at night, goes back in the daytime.'

'Just the one?' asked Marcie. 'I thought Sam said . . .'

'He did. Alice has got another folding bed she used to keep for Ruth when they went camping. She's asked Howard to bring it over later.'

'Howard?'

Karen was filling the kettle at the tap, ready to make coffee. 'He's the twins' dad. He's a great guy.' She laughed. 'A little weird, but great. I'm surprised you never met him.'

Marcie shrugged her shoulders. 'I don't know a lot about Sam, I guess. Family or nothing.'

'I'm sure you soon will,' Karen said, breezily.

Marcie stared at her. 'How come?'

'You're not going back to Montana are you? Not straight off, I mean.'

'No way! Sam said I should write my folks and I guess I will, but I'm going to tell them I'm staying here.' She felt herself blushing. 'Oh, I didn't mean . . .' She pointed to the floor. '. . . *here*. I just meant in the city. I'll find some place of my own, I guess.'

Karen spooned instant coffee into two mugs. 'It won't be easy, not till you've put some money by. It took me months and months to find my first place and then when I had to move out from there, months again. I was dead lucky to find this.'

Marcie's face had set in a frown.

'Hey!' said Karen. 'You can stay here for a spell, just as long as you don't mind the clutter. And remember, Alice said she could find you some work at the restaurant.'

'You sure she wasn't just saying that, I mean, for Sam's sake?'

'You really don't know Alice yet. She isn't like that at all. Wild horses couldn't drag words out of Alice she didn't want to say. No, she'll employ you as long as you work hard for as long as she needs you and no more. The fact that it'll please Sam is just a bonus as far as she's concerned. Sugar?'

'Two, please.'

'Sure.'

The two girls sat on the floor, leaning back against the walls.

'You and Sam,' Marcie said, eventually, 'you're going steady, I guess.'

Karen spluttered so hard into her coffee, Marcie thought she was going to choke.

'What did I say?'

'You know what you said. God! Don't ever let Sam hear you say that. He isn't going with anyone.'

Marcie sat back and sipped at her coffee.

'And you don't have to look so darned pleased about it,' said Karen, with a knowing grin.

Marcie just kept on sipping her coffee and said nothing; if there was a smile on her face, well, that wasn't her fault now, was it?

The restaurant was in that section of the city called Little Italy. Like most of the other places it served fresh pasta with any one of a dozen special sauces: spaghetti, tagliatelle, fettucine, rigatone, macaroni — any shape and thickness of pasta you might fancy.

There were a couple of tables outside on the street and fifteen or so inside — they were round and marble-topped with heavy iron legs. The walls of the restaurant had been painted with large murals of the Italian coast which had now faded; the tiles on the floor had begun to dip and crack at intervals.

Behind the counter which ran along one side, the espresso machine gurgled and gasped.

Michael Angelo sat at the rear, at his usual table, drinking his usual strong black coffee; his evening plate of Stufatine alla Romana before him. One of his cousins sat alongside him, a younger brother sat opposite. The tables to the right and in front of him also had his younger relations as customers, young and a little wild, the kind that were headstrong and sometimes overexcited, but good boys to have working for you.

Michael Angelo wiped the edges of his mouth with his napkin and smiled behind it. Headstrong boys to go around knocking heads.

He was happy with the way things were going. Pretty soon all those gangs would be under control and he would be running things again, the way his family had in the old days. The way his grandfather would walk right up to people and make them an offer they couldn't refuse.

Angelo laughed out loud and all of his brothers and cousins looked at him and laughed too, pleased that he was happy.

They were all so busy laughing that they failed to hear the four cars pull up, two outside the front entrance, two more at the rear. They were still laughing when Jackie Eves walked right into the restaurant, not pausing at the counter, carrying on down the aisle towards the back with Sam and Lennie backing her up and four plain-clothes officers behind them.

By now nobody was laughing.

Michael Angelo stood up, settling his shoulders inside his cashmere jacket. A ruby ring shone dully from the little finger of his left hand. 'What is this. . . ?' he began.

'Shut up!' the lieutenant snapped and, without turning her head, she said to Lennie. 'Well? Is he here?'

Lennie had already spotted the man from the

record store, sitting at the table to Angelo's right. He wasn't difficult to pick out — especially with a plaster stuck to the side of his face where he had been hit by a flying toaster.

'That's him,' said Lennie, stepping forward and pointing.

'You're sure?'

'Sure.'

'All right,' she said to her officers. 'Take him!'

The man jumped for the back door only to find it opened to him and a policewoman standing there with a revolver in her hand that was pointing directly at him.

'Hey, Angelo!' said Jackie Eves. 'Why don't you put your hands high while we're about it?'

'Why should I wish to do that?' asked Michael Angelo.

'For one thing, it'd stop you getting any ideas about reaching for that automatic you've got stashed away, making a bulge in that nice jacket of yours. And for another — you're under arrest.'

The twins were all for celebrating straight away, but Jackie Eves had known too many other occasions when the likes of Angelo had been arrested one moment and waltzed free the next. So at her suggestion they waited until the pre-trial arrangements had been gone through; until Lennie had gone along to the identification parade and sworn to his evidence — and until Fat Freddy was well enough to do the same. Now that Freddy realized that helping the police was the only way to get himself a light sentence, he gave them all the help they needed. He even persuaded his young friend, Neb, to do the same.

In the middle of all these weeks of waiting, Karen

172

happened to glance across at Marcie's guitar one evening in the flat and say, 'D'you ever get that thing out of its case, or are you planning to see how long it takes to decay in there?'

Right then, Marcie only grunted and gave no other response.

But the next time Karen came back from work to find Marcie alone, Marcie was picking some chords and trying to find the best rhyme to close off one of her lines. Marcie finally got it right while Karen made coffee; she sang and played the song and Karen applauded and the next day at the restaurant she had a few words with Alice.

In honour of Michael Angelo, whose picture was in the papers in the crime section, Alice arranged a special Italian-style meal. Jackie Eves was there, as were Armstrong Cutler and Jed Chambers. Howard sat with Sam and Lennie on either side of him, feeling proud. Ruth sat next to Karen and as for Marcie . . .

Well, Alice had cleared one corner of the room and found some wooden blocks to make a raised area like a stage.

'If this works out,' she had whispered to Marcie, 'we might have to see about making this more permanent. I always did think the one thing this place lacked was a little music.'

Jackie Eves ordered and opened a bottle of champagne and they all drank a toast to Sam and Lennie for continuing to help oil the wheels of justice.

And then it was Marcie's turn. She sat on a stool under a small spotlight and quietened the guests with a few chords of her guitar.

'This is for Sam and for Lennie as well,' she said. 'Though I'd be lying if I didn't say it was more specially for Sam. After all, it's thanks to him, mostly, that I'm sitting up here at all.'

She looked at the fingerboard of the guitar, hit the first chord and began to sing.

'Feeling like an east bound train,' she sang; 'Pulling through the snow.

'Used to think the only place I knew was lonely,' she sang: 'Now I know there are places with love in them and words that don't have to mean goodbye.'

BEAVER BOOKS FOR OLDER READERS

There are loads of exciting books for older readers in Beaver.
They are available in bookshops or they can be ordered directly
from us. Just complete the form below and send the right money
and the books will be sent to you at home.

☐	WATER LANE	Tom Aitken	£1.95
☐	FRANKENSTEIN	David Campton	£1.75
☐	IN THE GRIP OF WINTER	Colin Dann	£1.99
☐	TWISTED CIRCUITS	Mick Gowar	£1.75
☐	FANGS OF THE WEREWOLF	John Halkin	£1.95
☐	TEMPEST TWINS Books 1 – 4	John Harvey	£1.99
☐	YOUR FRIEND, REBECCA	Linda Hoy	£1.99
☐	REDWALL	Brian Jacques	£2.95
☐	THE GOOSEBERRY	Joan Lingard	£1.95
☐	WHITE FANG	Jack London	£1.95
☐	ALANNA	Tamora Pearce	£2.50
☐	A SHIVER OF FEAR	Emlyn Roberts	£1.95
☐	A BOTTLED CHERRY ANGEL	Jean Ure	£1.99
☐	THE MAGICIANS OF CAPRONA	Daina Wynne-Jones	£1.95

If you would like to order books, please send this form, and the
money due to:
ARROW BOOKS, BOOKSERVICE BY POST, PO BOX 29,
DOUGLAS, ISLE OF MAN, BRITISH ISLES. Please enclose
a cheque or postal order made out to Arrow Books Ltd for the
amount due including 22p per book for postage and packing
both for orders within the UK and for overseas orders.

NAME ....

ADDRESS ....

....

Please print clearly.